Deeper Than Destiny

Deeper Than Love, Book 1

...

EMMA ASHE

This is a work of fiction. Similarities to real people, places, or events are entirely coincidental.

...

DEEPER THAN DESTINY

First edition. November 13, 2018.

ISBN: 0-9998699-5-7

ISBN-13: 9780999869956

Written by Emma Ashe

www.emmaashe.com/books[1]

ALSO BY EMMA ASHE

Deeper Than Love

An Indecent Apposal

...

---

1. http://www.emmaashe.com/books/deeper

2. http://www.emmaashe.com/books/deeper

3. http://www.emmaashe.com/books/deeper

4. http://www.emmaashe.com/books/deeper

5. http://www.emmaashe.com/books/deeper

6. http://www.emmaashe.com/books/apposal

7. http://www.emmaashe.com/books/apposal

8. http://www.emmaashe.com/books/apposal

9. http://www.emmaashe.com/books/apposal

10. http://www.emmaashe.com/books/apposal

11. http://www.emmaashe.com/books/apposal

12. http://www.emmaashe.com/books/apposal

An Indecent Apposal Volume 1, Books 1-3[13]
An Indecent Apposal Volume 2, Books 4-6[14]

...

An Indecent Apposal Collection 1, Books 1-6[15]

Get notified of new releases & free reads:
www.emmaashe.com/signup[16]

13. http://www.emmaashe.com/books/apposal-set

14. http://www.emmaashe.com/books/apposal-set

15. http://www.emmaashe.com/books/apposal-set

16. http://www.emmaashe.com/signup

ACKNOWLEDGMENTS

This book wouldn't even be here without the encouragement of some of the finest writers I know. Thank you for cheering me on Skylar Hill and Cici Coughlin.

DEDICATION

For Tony

CHAPTER 1 | Finn

Four years ago...

And then I kiss her.

My hands go to her face, cupping her jaw and tilting her open for me. My hips grind into her, feeling the curves I've craved for years and making her gasp.

"Finn!"

It threatens to make my dick punch straight through my jeans. We've known each other almost our whole lives. She's said my name a million times, but this time? It damn near undoes me.

I kiss her again, giving her everything I have and then kissing her harder—and she matches me. Stroke for stroke. Touch for touch. Her leg slides up mine and I lift her to me. Her thighs tighten around my hips and she yanks me to her, pulling us even tighter together.

Even tighter into the heat between her legs.

We crash into the wall behind her and my eyes roll back as she grinds against me. She feels fucking amazing, fucking *perfect*.

And then she pulls back.

"Finn?" Her eyes are starry and her mouth is over-pink from my stubble. I can't stop staring at it even as alarm coils in my gut. Is she okay? Are *we* okay? Maybe I did this wrong?

"I want you," she whispers, sounding frantic. "I want you *now*."

It shouldn't be possible, but my dick goes even harder—and I still can't move. I should be all over her. I *want* to be all over her.

But I try to take a damn breath because this is Libby I'm kissing. Libby I want to take to bed.

Libby my best friend.

This is moving fast, I realize. Too fast? Definitely too fast. This is like a fucking whirlwind. For a second, I'm in my head and I'm freaking

7

out and then Libby's fingers tangle in my T-shirt, exploring me, and my skin goes hot. My brain blanks.

My brain never blanks.

"This isn't dating," she mutters. Reminding me? Reminding herself? I can't think straight. Everywhere she touches burns. "We're not strangers."

"God no." My voice has gone rough.

"I want you." Her eyes search my face, and for a moment, I'm blown away. She's impossibly lovely. I never get tired of looking at her. I never get tired of *being* with her.

"I thought you wanted me?" she whispers.

"More than anything."

And *now* I let myself explore: the line of her jaw...the sweep of her neck. It makes my mouth go dry.

She's so fucking perfect, I think and I want to tell her, but I can't seem to find my voice—and then she wiggles against me and pulls her tank top over her head, revealing the red lace bra underneath.

I suck in a breath, and then another. I can't look away from her and Libby grins like she knows it.

"Then satisfy me," she whispers.

Blood thumps in my dick nearly taking me to my knees. "Satisfy you?" I breathe, rubbing against her so I hit her clit and make her moan. "Fuck yes, but first I want to make you beg."

She gasps, eyes going bright with want.

"Do you like that?" I rub her again and earn another moan. Christ, I could listen to her to do that all damn day. "You are the hottest thing I have ever seen."

And I hold her tight against me, carrying her into her bedroom. Libby arches her back as I shove the door open. I cross to the bed and toss her down. For a second, it's like we're playing around and the tension evaporates. She bursts out laughing and it makes me laugh.

She's always been able to do that for me. Always.

I drag my T-shirt over my head and hear Libby gasp. Her gaze trails over my chest...slides down my stomach...and lingers on my belt.

No. My hard-on.

Holy shit. She's going to be the death of me, I realize and grin. "Like what you see?"

"I like being able to look at you openly"—a mischievous gleam enters her eyes—"not have to resort to peeking."

It's like the world spins around. All this time she was peeking at me? I was *definitely* peeking at her. "Spying on me?" I ask, voice finally returning to me. "Nice. Well, then fair's fair. Strip."

Color climbs Libby's cheeks, but she doesn't look away as her hands go to her jeans' top button.

I have waited for years to see this. Years. And to know she's watching me while I watch her? It's every fantasy I've ever had come to life.

She raises one dark brow, and pushes her jeans down, exposing gorgeous soft skin...and a red lace thong.

I scrub one hand over my mouth. Libby's the one who broke the ice and confessed her feelings for me. She said she didn't know how I'd react, but now it seems like she came prepared.

"Did you dress for me?" I finally manage.

She shakes her head, strands of dark hair spilling around her cheeks. She usually wears it up and now I can't wait to drag her ponytail down and run my fingers through all that silk. "I should probably say yes," she tells me that mischievous glint in her eyes again, "but...I like pretty lingerie. I wear it for me."

And thank God for that, I think. Libby has the kind of body born for lingerie. Her generous thighs slope upward into the most grabbable ass I have ever seen, her waist nips in, begging for me to kiss her sides (that I *know* are ticklish), and her lush breasts are barely contained in their lacey bra cups. Every time she breathes, they heave up, calling me—and then there's Libby, who's smiling again like she owns my ass.

She does, I realize because now her thumbs have hooked around the thong's edge and she's dragging it down an inch. "But if you like it..." she trails off and drags the thong down another inch. "If you like it, I could show you the other things I have."

Visions—Libby bent over in a black bustier, Libby naked except for silk stockings, Libby topless in lacey boyshorts—pummel me and I have to shake them off. I strip down as quickly as I can, crawl up the bed until I'm over her.

Until she's pinned.

"I've dreamed of fucking you." My voice doesn't even sound like my own. It's rough, ragged. It makes her lick her lips. "I've jerked off again and again with only you on my mind. And you know what?"

"What?" she whispers.

"You're even more amazing than my fantasies."

A shyness creeps into her expression, and for a beat, I think I've somehow said too much—and then her chin lifts. "And what are those fantasies?"

That's my Libby, I think, stuffing down my laugh. She never backs down. Ever. Not when we were ten and she dared me to jump off the garage roof, and damn sure not when we're half-naked and talking about what I want to do to her.

I grin. "You're soon to see," I say, sliding my hand down her side. Exploring her...learning her...*possessing* her.

"Tell me," she whispers.

And I can't stop my smile.

CHAPTER 2 | Finn

"Begging already?" I ask her, beyond delighted. Libby's blazing hot to the touch and growing hotter by the second. She loves how I tease her.

We both do.

"In one," I begin, watching her expression as I continue to explore her luscious curves, "you're bent over the edge of my bed and I've kissed and teased your nipples until you're aching, until every time they rub against my sheets, you moan." I pause, touching her and studying her and wanting her.

Do *not* fuck this up, Oliver, I tell myself and I circle my knuckle once more, enjoying her slick heat.

"Do you like me telling you that?" I ask and circle again because I can't help myself. She's so wet it nearly makes my eyes roll back into my head, and at my question, she grows even wetter.

She loves this too.

"Yes," she murmurs at last.

And I reward her with another circle, teasing and teasing.

Her back arches, shoving her gorgeous breasts into the air. "I love you telling me that," she pants. "Let's do it now."

"Really?" I rock my knuckle in her and nearly shout when her pussy spasms around me, needing more, *frantic* for more. "You want me to tease you until you ache? You want me to enter you from behind, stroking you until you're desperate for release?"

She gasps as I stroke her, my play making her wild. Desperate.

It's breathtaking to watch. But I'm not sure how much more I can take. My balls are actually aching now. My cock keeps straining against the cool sheets.

"Because I'd want to take my time with you," I continue, sliding my thumb ever so gently across her clit and willing my hard-on to chill. I'm not going to nut like some fucking teenager. "I've wanted this for too long not to enjoy every fucking second."

It's the damn the truth and my biggest secret and it should scare me shitless that I said it, but now that it's out there? It feels right.

Frighteningly right.

I tap her clit once and her head thrashes back and forth against the pillow, dark hair spilling everywhere. I'm driving her out of her mind and I still can't get enough.

"Take me fast," she pants, arching her back so her perfect breasts sway upward. "And *then* take me slow. Just take me."

That does it. I nearly come on the spot and have to close my eyes and think of baseball and golf and baseball and golf *statistics* to get a hold of myself. Someone far away is cursing.

And then I realize it's me.

Libby might be under me. I might have her wet and begging, but she's in control.

And I can't stop my grin.

"I know exactly what I want to do," I tell her and drop my mouth to hers, kissing her as desperately as I did before—and then breaking away. I ease my way down her gorgeous body, kissing her neck...her breasts...her stomach.

She wiggles into me, eyes sliding shut as I tug down her thong, kissing her skin as I pass. I yank the thong past her knees and fling the scrap of silk somewhere. I don't even look.

And then I push her legs apart.

Libby gasps, rocking up in surprise. Vaguely, I know she's staring me down and I should look up. I should smile at her and tell her something sexy.

But all my words have left me.

She's completely open to me and she's completely, fucking *perfect*.

I run my thumbs gently up and down her slick folds and she shudders, grinding into my hands, desperate for release. It leaves me in awe.

I look up at her. "You're so beautiful, do you know that?"

She blushes furiously, watching me as I watch her—and going wetter and wetter. I can feel her heat building against my hands, and when her hips move against me, searching for more, I know exactly how I'm going to give it to her. I lick my lips, unable to wait.

"Finn?"

I lower myself to her, mouth going straight to her heated core. I tongue her, tease her, take her straight to the edge so she's panting my name and begging me for release. Her hips jerk toward my mouth and I know what she needs—more pressure, more touching—and I pull back.

And hold her down.

Licking her until she soaked and aching.

She moans my name once more, an edge creeping into her tone. I know Libs, pinning her down like this should infuriate her, but it isn't. It's taking her higher.

And I'm fucking thrilled.

"Finn," she moans and I kiss the inside of her thigh, watch her core clench. She needs this. Her whole body is burning. "Please," she adds and now *I'm* burning too. I give her two fingers, rubbing her just right and then rubbing deeper, stroking her clit with my thumb. She grinds down on me, searching for more, and I can't take it. I have to give it to her.

"Come for me," I manage, my voice barely above a whisper.

She stirs, eyes heavy-lidded and more beautiful than ever. "What?"

I love seeing her like this. I love knowing I made her like this. "Come for me," I say, lifting my voice a little now, emphasizing the order. Her eyes fly wide open and I make sure she watches me lick her up and down. "Come now," I say and twirl my tongue around her clit.

Watching her.

It makes it even better for me—and for her when I feel her pussy clench around my fingers. She holds my gaze and it takes everything I have not to come.

"Now," I order and arc my fingers into her.

She comes in a rush, thrashing, screaming.

My name.

My name again and again and again as I pleasure her, pushing her over, taking everything she has until she's panting.

"Finn," she gasps. "Oh my God."

I laugh. That was fucking perfect. I want it again. "Again," I order and lick her clit.

She shudders against my mouth. "I can't." A ragged breath. "Not so soon."

"*Yes*, so soon." I lick her and she jerks, hips lifting toward my mouth again. I moan. She's so *fucking* perfect.

"Finn." She's reaching for me now and I slip from her hands, settling my tongue around her now incredibly sensitive clit. Every time I skim close, she arches off the bed. Every time I slide away, her hips follow, begging for more. "I'm too sensitive. I can't."

You can, I think and lick her again. Feel her melt. So fucking responsive. I want more, but I pull back, gently biting her inner thigh as I watch emotions chase across her face: surprise and relief and...

Want.

She swallows, already dark eyes going even darker as she realizes what I can do to her.

What I *will* do to her—if she'll only let me. Christ, I hope she lets me.

I skim my knuckles around her tender skin and she melts into me once more. "Again," I tell her.

And she comes like it's a command.

CHAPTER 3 | Finn

Libby comes down like I've shattered her. She rolls over, breathing hard and fast. Her eyes swing briefly to me and then immediately away, like things are still too intense.

I get that. Looking at her right now, I feel like my chest's just cracked. My dick is straining hard enough to hurt, but it's like it's happening to someone else because I can't stop staring at her.

Like a freak, I realize and shift onto my back, giving her some space. To my delight, Libby rolls closer, turning onto her side and running her hand down my stomach.

And then lower.

"Can I...?" she whispers and the want in it makes my dick damn near stand up straight.

I fold my hand over hers, pinning it tight against my stomach. "No way. First time I come with you? I'll be buried inside you."

She shivers, eyes going starry again. Briefly, I think I might have gone too far and then she says, "We need a box of condoms. Let's go."

I nearly burst out laughing. "You want to leave already? I didn't do my job right." I grin up at her ceiling, trying—and failing—to slow my breathing. The girl is like a shot of adrenaline. I have blue balls for days, but I still feel like I'm flying.

"Oh, but you *did* do a good job." She sinks into the mattress, snuggling closer to me. It feels fucking fantastic even if I'm afraid to touch her anymore. My dick is still a hairsbreadth away from coming. "You did a *great* job. I don't think I've ever been this relaxed."

I don't think I've ever been that hard. My brain still feels foggy. "I had no idea you were so..."

I realize how that sounds only *after* it escapes my mouth, and for about a nanosecond, I think Libby's sex bliss is going to save me.

Then she flips over and I can feel her laser gaze bore into me. "So *what?*"

"So uninhibited." It's the truth, but it sounds cheesy as hell. I shake myself and look at her. "So brave. You knew what you wanted and you took it."

She smirks. "I took *you.*"

"You fucking did." I had no idea she wanted me like this, no idea she wanted me at all. It's mind-blowing.

Then she runs her fingertips up my chest and I realize there's a lot to Libby that's mind-blowing, like the way she's touching me right now. "You make me brave," she says softly. "Wanting this...made me brave."

I grab her hand and lift it to my mouth, kissing her knuckles. "You make me brave too."

She does too. She always has and I've always known it and now...

"I mean, you always have, right?" I clear my throat and pretend I'm interested in looking around her bedroom. My eyes skip from the black and white pictures she's covered one whole wall in to the shelf full of showjumping trophies. "You kick my ass whenever I need it. Remember that college interview I wanted to blow off?"

Libby grimaces. "How could I forget? I thought I was going to have to drag you in there."

Honestly? She would've. Thankfully, it didn't come to that, but only by the narrowest of margins. After finding out I was up for early admissions to Harvard, my dad had freaked. It was nothing but talks about making the family proud and living up to expectations—which were really just code for making *him* proud and living up to *his* expectations.

By the time Libby caught up with me, I was on a three-day bender, medicating my panic attacks with booze. No surprise it wasn't helping, but I couldn't seem to stop. Then she got there and my world re-centered.

"You can do this," she'd told me as we'd staggered to the master bathroom. She'd opened the shower door and shoved me under the water. Coldest moment of my life.

Lowest moment of my life—and she was there.

"Don't let your brain get in the way of what your heart knows you want," she'd said and for a second, I actually managed a smile. No one had ever put it like that and it was so true. Then and now, I've always felt like my brain is trying to kill me.

I'd taken her hand and pressed her palm against my chest and I knew she felt my racing heart when her face softened. She looked like I'd broken her.

Or worse, disappointed her.

"I'm scared shitless," I'd muttered, staring at the water circling my feet and the drain. "I hate feeling like this. I hate being this guy."

"Finn." Her voice had wavered like it did whenever she was about to cry. "Look at me."

It had taken everything I had to.

"You got this," she'd said.

"I don't feel like I do."

"That's because your head is lying to you right now." She'd tried to make it funny, but we both knew it was true and it was horrible.

Water had kept getting in my face, blurring her and smearing her, and I still couldn't look away. I'd needed to see if she was lying to me and...she wasn't.

"I'll believe in you until you can believe in yourself," she'd added.

I hadn't been able to manage a single word. No one, then or now, has ever believed in me like Libby believes in me.

And for probably the billionth time in the twelve years I'd known her, I'd wanted to kiss her. I'd wanted to pull her into the shower and never let her go.

I'd settled for a towel

And now you're in bed, I think, focusing on the ceiling fan so I can get the courage to say, "You're the one who's always believed in me. Always."

She goes quiet, gaze pinned to her bedroom's floor-length windows, and for few beats, I get to enjoy naked, warm Libby squeezed in next to me—and then she sits up, fingers pulling at the tangles in her hair. "Oh, I bet you do this all the time."

"You know I don't." Briefly, I'm confused and then I realize she's making this lighter. It's to help me. Somehow I'm sure of it. But I'm not going to let her dismiss this—especially with a dig a me being a slut. "Man-whoring has never been my problem."

"Yeah. True."

"Spend the weekend with me," I say, studying the pictures of Libby's best friends, Ally and Laurel, that are hanging above her desk. I'm trying for casual and doing a great job for someone whose entire insides are suddenly knotted. Don't say no, I pray. Don't say no.

"We live together."

It's true, of course. I've been living with Libby since my dad threw me out a few months ago, but that's not what I mean and she knows it. I turn to her and she's grinning.

"We're *already* spending the weekend together," she adds.

Again, she's making this light and it's anything but. I hold her gaze and say, "You know what I mean. Let me take you out. Let's see where this..." My words dry up. There's too much at stake.

"Goes?" Libby finishes and her voice turns it into a squeak.

"Exactly."

And it's like the air sucks out of the room. Libby stares at me and...trembles. She feels it too, I realize, but before I can say anything, she whips up a devilish—and familiar—smile. Wherever she wants this weekend to go, I will not be able to help, but to follow.

"I want it to go to the drugstore for condoms," she says.

I grin. "I want it to go back to bed." And I grab her, I drag her down to me, rubbing her bare breasts against my chest and enjoying her delighted gasp. I can't keep my hands off her. I rub down her shoulder blades...down her spine...I cup her ass and urge her close so I can whisper, "I want your pretty legs spread for me. I want you moaning. I want to hear you scream my name again."

She goes boneless. Hot.

She wants more, I realize and triumph punches through me.

Libs looks down at me. "I want..."

And I give it to her.

It feels like the beginning of everything. Libby is perfect and she's mine and in less than forty-eight hours everything will be ruined.

CHAPTER 4 | Libby

Now...

I'm not sure what I expected to see when I walked out of the stable that morning, but Finn Oliver wasn't it. It had been four years. Four. Years.

And now he was back.

Waiting for me, I realize and it turns my mouth dry—and spikes my temper. How *dare* he show up like this. After what he *did*. After how long it's *been*.

I'm stomping toward him even before I realize I'm moving and I can see something zing across his eyes. It better be panic, I think, but I know it's not. Past four years notwithstanding, I've known Finn my whole life. We were best friends, and for one weekend, we were lovers. I know when he wants something—or in this case, someone.

And honestly that just infuriates me even more.

I stomp faster and he leans one hip against his car door, watching me approach and looking like he just fell out of a high-end magazine ad. The guy is mind-scramblingly beautiful.

But I'm immune now, I remind myself. *I'm immune. I'm immune. I'mimmune!*

I stop and we're toe-to-toe. The Libby from four years ago would be noticing he still smells amazing, but the Libby from today is immune. Or mostly immune. "You have a lot of nerve showing up here like this, Finn."

He shrugs. "Didn't think you'd take my calls."

"You were right."

He shrugs again. "Can we talk? Privately?"

I start to say 'no' and then hesitate. I look up and down him and that's my *first* mistake. He's leaner than he was when I knew him and not in a good way. He looks like he's been sick.

Or stressed.

Then I look at his face and that's my *second* mistake. Finn is gorgeous. Honestly, Finn has *always* been gorgeous—he's pouty lips and a hard-lined jaw and hair you want to run your fingers through—but there are dark shadows under his eyes now and his skin is far too pale underneath his five o'clock stubble. He doesn't look well and I can't bring myself to ignore it.

Ugh, you're such a pain, I tell myself, sighing. I really hate myself sometimes. "Fine. But you better be quick. My dad's home and I don't want him seeing you."

"Why—"

"Don't do that. You know why. You started working for your dad right after my dad got pushed out. Kinda hard not to see the coincidence."

He hesitates, something I can't read churning in his expression, something I don't *want* to read. He opens his mouth and I hold up my hand. "Ten minutes. Max."

"It'll only take five."

Whatever. I try not to grind my teeth and turn back for the stable, waving for him to follow. It's not that I want him in my stable, but I damn sure don't want him out in the yard where my dad could see him. I can't even imagine how that conversation would go.

Correction: I don't want to imagine how that conversation would go.

For a nanosecond, Finn hesitates and then dashes after me. We duck into the stable and I pray he doesn't notice all the ways things have fallen down around here. The family farm used to be gorgeous now it's...rough.

Yeah, the brick aisleway is clean, but it's also super stained from years of use. The overhead rafters are patched and there's rust on the stall door hinges. If you go outside, there's fencing that needs repairing and a farm truck that needs replacing and...well...we look shabby.

It's thanks to him and his family, but I can't help but be embarrassed and *that* makes the whole thing even worse.

And one glance at Finn and I know he's already seen it all.

My stomach cramps and I cross both arms over my chest. "What do you want?"

"I have a problem at work."

"Oh?" I'm trying for disinterested and polite and, hopefully, 'I have no idea what you're talking about,' even though I absolutely do because Finn's dad had a meltdown on Twitter and it's all over social media. You can't get away from it.

Which is probably a good thing in many ways because people aren't going to let Mr. Oliver get away with it—and I have to admit a big part of me is thrilled. My dad never got justice, and yeah, a bunch of keyboard warriors won't make that happen either, but at least they're holding Finn's dad accountable.

"Maybe you've heard about it on the news." Finn's eyes are hunting my face like he's looking for secrets and it makes my neck go hot. "Maxon used our company Twitter handle to voice some really disgusting opinions about a former employee. It's been...tense."

I nod. "I bet. Oliver Holdings is known for two things: charity work and your father's tantrums—and those tantrums outshine anything you're doing in the charity world." I blink. Holy cow, I can't believe I said that.

Finn blinks like he can't believe I said it either. "Pretty much exactly."

Something shifts behind his eyes, a flash of connection, and a memory slams into me. Suddenly, we're not in my family's stable anymore.

We're in my apartment. Finn's has pinned me against the wall and I'm loving it.

And I'm also scared to death because this is my best friend *and* the guy I've been in love with since I was a kid. I'd run into the bathroom just seconds before to splash cold water on my face, to get myself together, and now Finn's holding me close and studying my face like he's looking for cracks.

"I was trying to get myself together," I'd explained and he had paused, something incredibly worried and earnest creeping into his eyes.

"You don't have to be 'together' for me," he had whispered.

"Yes, I do." Then I'd leaned in for a kiss, leaned in so close our lips almost touched. "I want to be together so you can take me apart."

A flash of heat rips through my body and I'm back and I'm shaking. This isn't four years ago, I remind myself. This is now. "So," I begin, deeply grateful my voice doesn't go rough, "what does this have to do with me?"

"I'm going to call a press conference tomorrow. I'm planning on apologizing for his behavior, discussing how we're going to prevent such behavior in the future, but I want to take it a step farther. I want to do some community outreach."

My heart double-thumps. Community outreach? Is he thinking about...? I don't let myself finish the thought. "Such as?"

"Such as I give you a hundred thousand for your therapy program and in exchange we get good publicity."

"A hundred *thousand* dollars?"

"Yeah." He looks around the stable aisle, gaze flicking from my stained brick to the patched rafters. "Looks like you could use it."

I hate him. The pity that made me give him a few minutes of my time evaporates in a flash. All I can remember now is that he ruined my father and made me cry and ghosted without a word of good-bye.

"No answer?" he asks and there's genuine fear in his eyes. He screwed up with that little comment and he knows it. "Am I to assume this means you're going to pass?"

I should say yes. This is the man who broke my heart, who helped his father destroy my family.

But when I look in his eyes, I see begging—desperation—and I know I can name my price. Thanks to Finn Oliver and his father, my family farm is falling down. Thanks to Finn Oliver and his father, our fortunes are about to change.

"Oh, no. No, not at all." I give him my brightest smile. "You want to pay me to make you look good? Barely possible, but you make it two-fifty and you're on."

He grins and unease curls through me. He always loved it when you negotiated, I think. Change your mind. Now.

But I don't get a chance because Finn says, "It's a deal."

CHAPTER 5 | Libby

"You're never going to believe what I just agreed to," I tell my best friends, sliding into the booth at our favorite Atlanta restaurant for breakfast. The air is heavy with the smell of coffee and pancakes and it's seriously making me reconsider my usual omelet. I take a deep breath and give the girls my best smile. "I'm going to work for Finn Oliver."

Laurel and Ally look at each other like I've just spoken in tongues. Honestly? It would probably make more sense if I had. Finn and I have history and none of it is good.

Okay, some of it is good.

It was good when we were growing up and had each other to lean on. It was good in college when I helped him with his panic attacks and he helped me with my accounting homework.

But I know my best friends aren't thinking about any of that.

"Wait." Ally's head slowly tilts as the full effect of what I just said occurs to her. "You're going to work for him? For Dickhead?"

Two older women turn around and glare at us. I give them an embarrassed little wave and hunch down into my seat. "Do you hear yourself?" I hiss.

"Do you hear *yourself*? He's an asshole!" Ally grips her butter knife like she's getting ready to go stab him. If I weren't so worried she *would* stab him, I would laugh. It's just such an incongruous image. Ally dresses like a flower girl. She's all drapey white lace in the summer and drapey white cashmere in the winter. There are usually tiny vintage gold rings woven into her braids and her fingernail polish veers from pale pink to paler pink.

"He made you cry for months!" she adds.

"Yeah," I say softly. "He did." He was also my oldest, dearest friend, my longest crush, and made me come so hard I could barely remember my own name. Not that I'm thinking about Finn in that way.

Okay, not that I'm thinking about it much.

Bottom line, losing sex like that was awful. But losing my best friend in the world? It was worse. My heart was broken and the person I wanted to call and cry to? Was Finn. The person who'd broken me in the first place.

I dump four packets of sweetener into my coffee and stir. "I need the money, okay? He's offering me a two hundred and fifty *thousand* to help make his firm look good."

The girls are back to blinking and staring at me. *I get that*, I think, taking a big swallow of coffee. *Ick. Needs more sweetener.*

Laurel frowns delicately, the skin between her brows pleating. If Ally is our resident hippie, Laurel's always been the new age yogi one of us. She opened a yoga studio straight out of college and now does in-person classes for about a hundred dedicated students and web classes for about a hundred thousand more. She's wildly successful and still every bit as down to earth as she was in college.

She also won't give her opinion unless asked. Even when it's eating her to death, which clearly it is at the moment. She looks at me, presses her mouth thin, and says nothing.

"I can tell you're thinking," I say, smiling. "Spit it out."

"I heard something about the firm not doing well. His dad took to Twitter and had some sort of rant?"

"Pretty much. It's tanking everything."

"Good," Ally says, shrugging one shoulder. It makes her slouchy blouse fall down her arm and she shoves it back into place. "After what they did to your family, I hope the Olivers go bankrupt. It would be perfect justice."

I try to say something nice and...I can't. She's right. It *would* be perfect justice. After my father was fired from Oliver Holdings, he was shattered. He had helped Finn's dad build the company from the ground up. They were partners.

Except they weren't really. Finn's dad put up all the capital and he kept all the company stock. Technically, everything belonged to him, but my dad worked and cared for the company like it was his own.

And then Finn came along and suddenly my dad was gone. It didn't make any sense. I mean, my dad was an amazing partner—and Finn? Finn had always said he didn't want to be anything like Mr. Oliver and then suddenly he was following in his footsteps.

I remember wondering if it had all been a horrible act, some involved lie he'd told me.

But then I started to wonder if something even worse was going on because my dad couldn't find another position. It was like he had been black-balled—not that he let on to my mom or me. We were clueless and he moved forward with my therapeutic riding center like everything was fine. And it wasn't. It *so* wasn't. I'm lucky he got me going, but it isn't enough to *stay* going, and four years later, I need a major influx of cash. It isn't just the farm that needs repairs. I need another therapy horse. I need to pay the insurance, which is astronomical considering all the ways people and horses can get hurt being around each other. The list goes on and on.

In some ways, Finn's appearance couldn't be better timed.

Ally crushes her napkin in her fist. "So what exactly are you supposed to do to 'make his firm look good'?"

"We're supposed to talk about it tonight."

Laurel sits up straighter. "Tonight? Like a date?"

"Not like a date."

Our favorite waitress, Louisa, hurries past our table. She looks at me. "Omelet?"

"Yes, please!"

She grins, heading toward another set of customers. The Bread and Butterfly is always packed on weekend mornings, but today it's especially crowded and Louisa is flying to keep up.

I turn back to the girls. "It's more like an opportunity to plan what we're going to do to"—I twist my voice so it sounds like Ally—"'make his firm look good.'"

I'm trying for a laugh, but I don't get one. The girls still look a half-second away from, dragging me home with one of them, and not letting me go until I can swear I'm over Finn Oliver.

Which I already am, but still.

"He bought you a horse," Ally says—like I needed the reminder. After Finn ghosted, the horse I'd wanted (but had no longer been able to afford to purchase) had showed up at our farm. Sceptre is everything I dreamed she'd be.

And Finn bought her for me.

I still don't know how he found the money. Maybe from his app sale? In the months that followed our break-up, I'd Googled him every day, hoovering up any information I could find. But there wasn't much to find beyond business news: he'd sold his app for a small fortune, started working for Oliver Holdings, and then Oliver Holdings became even more successful. There should've been more to find—a Facebook page, an Instagram account—but nope. It was like work absorbed him completely.

I nod vigorously. "He *did* buy me a horse. Your point?"

Ally leans across the table, eyes narrowed. "That's like diamonds for the rest of us normal people. Big diamonds."

I laugh. I can't help it. Ally and Laurel have never understood my obsession with horses and riding. They support it and they're happy for me, but I once heard Ally tell Laurel she couldn't understand the appeal of an animal that was known to kick *and* bite.

"He's not buying me a horse," I tell them. "He's paying to stand next to me while I do something good for the world. You know what the program means to me—what it means to the kids."

"Of course," Ally says, her eyes softening. "Don't get me wrong, the money is amazing, but..."

Laurel nods. "Exactly. But it's Finn."

"I can handle this." I smile at them. They glower at me. I smile wider. They...still glower at me. "I know what I'm doing," I add

"Honey." Laurel stirs another packet of sweetener into her coffee, watching me with huge, sad eyes. "When it comes to Finn Oliver, you can't be trusted."

CHAPTER 6 | Finn

"I don't get it," Merrick says, slouching lower on my couch. He's wearing the same clothes he was wearing yesterday and I'm not sure if he slept at the office because he's stressed or if he slept at the office because his latest girlfriend threw him out.

"Don't get what?" I ask.

"Since when do you get jumpy about a business meeting?"

"I'm not."

"You are. You've redone your tie four times."

"I haven't."

"Have."

I glare at him and he points to my chest. I glance down. Yep. My fingers are tangled in my silk tie's knot. Damn. I drop my hands, take a deep breath. Usually, it's Merrick charging around when he's stressed.

"I love what you've done with the place," he adds, throwing a meaningful look at my blank walls, or maybe my blank bookcases. It's all pretty much the same. "How long have you been living here again?"

"Two years? No. Almost three." I bought the condo on a whim. We have company apartments and I'd lived in them off and on during college, but I wanted something that was separate from the company.

More specifically, I wanted something my dad couldn't throw me out of.

"It's a crash pad," I explain. "It doesn't have to be nice."

"It *is* nice. It just looks like no one lives here." He glances around again, frowning. "Seriously, dude. It's almost creepy. I've seen more personality in hotels."

"You *would* know a lot about that." Merrick's man-whoring is almost legendary. I'm just grateful he never considers anyone at the office.

Merrick grins at me. "Rule One: never let them know where you live."

"Such a class act."

His grin widens. "Like your deal is any better? If you want to sleep with a woman, you practically make her sign a contract."

An exaggeration, but not by much. I think it's cleaner that way. I don't do relationships—not anymore. But a weekend here? Yeah. A date to a company function there? Sure. I don't have time for anything deeper.

And honestly, I don't want it.

"Rule Two," Merrick continues, using one of the financial reports to emphasize his point. "Let *them* get attached. *You* never get attached."

"Fascinating." And possibly bull shit. Or maybe not because Merrick's current conquest is a leggy blond who's almost as steely-eyed as he is. He might think he has the upper-hand—and he usually does—but something tells me Brynn has her agenda and it's probably closer to mine than he will ever realize.

That could be fun to watch, I think. I swipe the financial report out of Merrick's fist and flip to the forecasting data we're supposed to be reviewing, trying to wrench my head around and focus.

Merrick kicks my foot, unwilling to let it go. "I feel like I should know this, but...what do you do when you're not working?"

"I work some more." I check the time on my phone. Almost two hours before I'm supposed to meet Libby. Even with Atlanta traffic, if I leave now, I'll be way early. I frown and toss the cell on top of my laptop bag.

The screen lights up with another Twitter notification. I try not to look, but I still catch a glimpse of our company's handle and 'hypocrite.' And it shouldn't sting...

But it does.

When I went to work for my dad, I headed up new project development, but I also got involved with our company's marketing team and we started looking at outreach opportunities. I started with the usual stuff—checks to the High Museum in Atlanta, the Boys and Girls Club—and then we started narrowing our focus, donating money to schools and therapy programs for kids. It was real, it was personal, and my dad made the whole thing look like nothing more than another company's marketing stunt after he went public with his tantrum.

"You're doing it again," Merrick says, not looking up. "Seriously. What's the deal?"

I force my hands back down from my tie. "Too much caffeine," I lie.

"Then back it down. We need this to work."

Understatement of the century. I take another deep breath, trying to fend off how my chest wants to shrink, and flick through some of the paperwork Merrick brought. Usually, we review the bi-monthly finance reports in one of the offices at Oliver Holdings, but he wanted a change of pace from listening to the protesters and came here.

"It'll work," I tell him, settling on the chair across from him. "No one can resist cute ponies and cuter kids."

"What the hell's a pony?" Merrick asks.

"It's a little horse."

"Jesus, rich people." His eyes roll. "First, little dogs and now little horses."

He's kidding. Sort of. Merrick and I work well together. Our brains work similarly and we're both driven as hell, but we didn't grow up the same way. At all.

Not that we've actually shared a whole lot of family details. Merrick doesn't say much about his and I damn sure don't say anything about mine, but it only takes a Google search to figure out who my dad is and he's made some assumptions. Can't blame him really.

When I signed on for working for Oliver Holdings, Merrick eagerly followed me and I really couldn't blame him. Working for a Fortune 500 and directly reporting to *the* Maxon Oliver? I'm sure it sounded like a dream job. It's not even close though—and he learned quickly enough after watching my father grow increasingly paranoid over the past four years.

The Twitter tirade just scrapes the surface of what we've been dealing with behind the scenes, and if it were just me, I would let my father burn the company to the ground.

But it isn't just me. It's about four hundred employees and their families all hanging in the balance.

It's also Libby and her dad.

Not that they know it.

"Everyone loves pint-sized stuff," I remind Merrick. "Trust me. You'll thank me later."

My partner opens his mouth—with some smart-ass response no doubt—and then snaps it shut. He cocks his head, listening to something and I'm about to ask what when faint shouting reaches my ears. Faint, *repetitive* shouting.

Fuck.

"Protestors," Merrick mutters.

I stride to one of the ceiling-high windows and look down. Sure enough, in spite of the late November chill, a semi-circle of protestors has gathered around my building's entrance. My chest—already tight—rachets even tighter.

"I'm going to hear that chant in my fucking dreams for the rest of my life," he continues, flipping through the financial reports.

"It's kinda catchy," I say, my breath fogging up against the cold window. Six stories below us, a white van pulls up close to the protestors and parks. Unease prickles through me.

"Don't start. They get one *whiff* of you agreeing with them and it'll be blood in the water."

It would be too. Oliver Holdings would get ripped apart even more—and my father would be furious. He wouldn't take it out on me, not directly. He'd go straight for Libby and her father.

"At least, it can't get any worse," Merrick says.

I watch as the white van's side door opens and two guys with cameras spill out. They make a bee-line for the protestors, cameras propped on their shoulders. "Hey, Merrick?"

"Yeah?"

"It just got worse."

CHAPTER 7 | Libby

I've been trying on clothes for the better part of an hour and I'm still no closer to figuring something out.

Just pick something, I tell myself, scanning the floor of my bedroom. It looks like my closet threw up—my clothes, Laurel and Ally's clothes, clothes I don't even remember buying. This is ridiculous.

I'm ridiculous.

I stuff down a groan and dip into the pile closest to my feet, finding a black long-sleeved knit dress. It's Laurel's and it could definitely work. I'd just need...I turn back to the bed and find a pair of black tights on a pillow and my black boots under some T-shirts.

That's a lot of black, I think. Try it anyway.

I tug everything on and study my reflection. I still don't like it. This isn't the right dress. Maybe I shouldn't even wear a dress. Maybe this is a pants-type business meeting.

Pants-type?

I scowl at myself. I don't usually worry too much about my clothes. When I'm at the barn, the horses don't care and the kids don't notice. Not to mention there's the whole dirt/manure/dust thing. The only time people wear nice clothes to the stables is when they're in a Ralph Lauren ad.

But I want to look cute for my meeting with Finn—*not* because I want him to find me sexy, but because I want to feel confident.

Right? Right. I scowl even deeper, strip off everything and stomp to my underwear draw. I pull out my favorite lace bustier and matching panties, wiggle into them and then reach for thigh high silk stocking. They slide effortlessly up my legs and I pin them to my garter belt. I turn back to my mirror.

There. Confidence.

Now it almost doesn't matter what I wear. Even so my fingers are itching to dial Laurel or Ally—or Laurel *and* Ally. They know my closet as well as they know their own. They could put together something in a snap.

But they'd also want to know why I was worrying.

I frown, tugging the black dress over my head again. Correction: they would *already* know why I was worrying.

I shake my hair loose and run my fingers through it, studying my reflection and debating whether I should do something with it. My eyes drift from my tangles and snag on the picture I took of Brody and Bridget Macken. Technically, they're not with my therapy program, but I give them riding lessons and they're the cutest twins ever. Brody once told his uncle that I was quite the 'ball-buster' (Brody has a potty mouth) and his uncle told me and remembering that?

It kinda makes me feel like one. I can do this.

"Honey?" My mom's voice drifts up the stairwell. My apartment is on the farm, up above the stables and a few minutes' walk from the main house. It's tiny—I mean, you can literally hear someone call my name from the downstairs tack room—but it's perfect for me. "Are you okay?"

"Fine!" I grab my boots and a bright red scarf from my desk and dash out of my bedroom and down the hallway. The main house is a 1900s restored low-country farm house, but the stable is much more recent addition. The apartment I live in is a kitchen/sitting room, bathroom, and bedroom, and unlike most of the property around it, four years of struggle hasn't made much dent. The walls are still covered in colorful family pictures and the bookshelves are crowded with my old trophies and ribbons. For a second, it feels like everything is okay.

For a second, it feels like I'm still in college and running to meet Finn.

I shove the thought away and thunder down the stained-wood stairs. Mom meets me by the last step, grinning. "You look really nice," she says, giving me a hug. This close, I can see how the once faint lines around her eyes have grown deeper. She looks permanently worried these days. "Will you be late?"

"No, not at all. Just meeting the girls. Laurel has a new guy." I'm smiling like everything great, but inwardly cringing. I hate lying to her, but the alternative isn't going to work either.

In my haste to nail Finn to the wall, I hadn't considered logistics. My parents are going to want to know how I found the money to repair our farm and keep my therapy program going and *I'm* going to need a good explanation.

One that doesn't involve Oliver Holdings.

So far, I don't have anything.

"Walk me back to the house?" Mom asks, linking her arm through mine. We step into the chill evening and hurry up toward my childhood home. "Have you met the new guy?" she asks.

"Not yet."

"I hope he's nice. She's a lovely girl. So calm."

"It's all the yoga."

"Maybe I should try it."

I grin. "She would love that." It's the truth too. Laurel's always trying to recruit more people. She's been trying to get me to do yoga for years, but thanks to the farm, I rarely have the time.

We take the backdoor into the kitchen and the smell of spaghetti sauce and garlic bread hits me, making my stomach clench. Mom always goes Italian when stressed. "Anything you want to tell me before I go?"

The corner of her mouth twitches. She's either about to smile or about to cry.

"Mom?"

"Is it that obvious?"

"No!" I pause. "Maybe a little?" She studies me, trying to work out how I knew she was upset and I cave. "You're cooking Italian," I explain. "You only do that when you're melting down."

"Oh." Her mouth twitches again and this time, she smiles. "I'll try to be more imaginative next time."

I start to say 'Don't be' or 'Tell me what's wrong,' but none of it comes out because suddenly she's squeezing my hand and looking at me with tears in her eyes. "I heard you talking to Laurel the other day. I didn't mean to eavesdrop, but I heard you say you might have to close the therapy program down."

I take a shaky breath. Until Finn showed up, it was a distinct possibility. "We're not there yet. I have a few more ideas."

She flinches like I'm lying to her—worse, like I'm lying to myself and I'm not. I'm *not*.

"Mom, we're making real progress. Did I tell you about how Ian is interacting more? He's—"

"Honey, what if this isn't what you're supposed to do with the rest of your life? What if losing the therapy program is actually for the best?"

For a second, I feel like I'm watching us from three-stories up above. I can't believe she just said that. I can't believe she would *think* that. "What?" I finally manage.

"You're killing yourself to make this work. What if it's not *supposed* to work? There's a reason these programs struggle to stay afloat."

I stiffen. This should be the part where I argue about how it's nearly impossible to keep them afloat because it's nearly impossible to make them *affordable*. Between insurance costs and horse costs, it's a financial black hole and probably a terrible decision because no one gets rich doing this stuff.

But you can be fulfilled. You can make a difference in the world.

This is my calling. It's what I'm supposed to do with my life.

She places one hand on my arm and squeezes. "I don't want you to miss out on your future."

It's so gentle, but it still threatens to take me apart. Losing the therapy program would be like losing part of myself—a crucial part.

"I won't miss out on my future." And I wish I could tell her that after tonight, I'll be one step closer.

CHAPTER 8 | Finn

Turns out, finding a place to meet Libby was a good deal harder than I expected. Merrick usually takes potential clients to the St. Regis for drinks before contract review, but Libby isn't a client and I'm pretty sure taking her to one of Atlanta's nicest hotels implies I expect to sleep with her.

After way more obsessing than I would ever admit, I ended up sending her the address to The Hole In The Wall, a locals' bar close to her family's place. I'm not sure taking her to a bar is any better than taking her to a hotel, but I know she'll be familiar with it and there's less than a zero chance of us being spotted together.

Which is apparently more of a concern now than it was even twelve hours ago. I glance in my rear-view mirror again. No white van in sight. The guys who owned it were reporters or film students or...something. I hadn't really caught the whole story because as soon as I walked out of my building, one of them shoved his camera in my face and started yelling about my father's beliefs.

For about a second, it pasted me to the spot and then I shoved past, climbed into my car—that'll teach me to park street-side for a while—and took off. They retaliated by following, trailing me for a couple of miles before I gunned it through a changing light and left them behind.

Of course, now thanks to all the lead-foot driving, I'm a full thirty minutes early to meeting Libby.

Loads of time to obsess, awesome, I think, pulling into Senoia. It's a tiny—and quintessentially southern town—on the southside of Atlanta. I park by one of the gift shops, maybe a block from the Hole In The Wall, and take a couple minutes to breathe.

It doesn't work. I still want to punch something until it breaks.

"Fuck it," I mutter and get out. An icy wind blasts me and I stuff my hands into my pockets and turn for the bar. Technically, this isn't my first time at The Hole In The Wall. Libby brought me once or twice in college. It's tucked downstairs from a swanky southern restaurant. With a dimly-lit sign above a narrow staircase leading down to the door, you'd miss it if you didn't know it was there.

Thanks to the growing winter dark, the lights are already blazing inside. High top tables are scattered around the main floor, a huge oak bar lines one entire wall, and the walls...well, the walls are covered with taxidermied animals—raccoons, deer, squirrels. This isn't exactly uncommon for certain parts of the south. But these animals are all in costume—and usually wearing hats.

"Table for one?" a hostess asks me and I try not to focus on the grinning—snarling?—warthog by her head. I can't tell if he's happy with his lot or wants to eat my face.

"Two," I say and she leads me to one of the booths. I like that. A lot. Allows me to put my back to the wall and watch the rest of the place. I'm still not sure where I picked up that habit, but Libby—because of course it was Libby—pointed it out right before we graduated.

"Anything to drink while you wait?" the hostess asks me.

"Yeah, beer. Whatever you have on tap."

She shrugs and turns away, leaving me to cool my heels, and briefly it feels like it's four years ago and I'm waiting on Libby to meet me so we can have a drink and laugh. That was before she told me she wanted me, before I told her I'd wanted her for years, before my dad made me leave her.

I swallow and yank myself back to the present. And excellent timing too because Libby walks through the door and everything in me—*everything*—strings tight.

She's wearing over-the-knee black suede boots that hug her gorgeous legs, a long-sleeved black dress that hugs her generous curves, and an oversized red scarf that's still fluttering a bit from the outside wind. She says something to the hostess who turns and points at me.

I have the ridiculous urge to wave, but since I'm not twelve, I stuff it down, nursing my beer as she thanks the woman and pats the warthog.

"I'm surprised you remember this place," she says, sliding into the chair across from me. My hand jerks toward her—a stupid muscle memory leftover from when we were more—and I sweep my palm over the tabletop. "Why did you want to come so far south?"

"Easier for you." It's the truth, but now that it's out there I wish I hadn't said it. Something zings through Libby's eyes and I can't read it. Doubt starts to scratch at me. I can feel my chest funneling shut.

"Did you order anything?" she asks, turning her attention to the laminated menu. "Because I'm starved."

"You're always starved." Another truth and another time I wish I hadn't said it. It's like my brain can't separate what *was* from what's *now*.

And Libby looks at me like she knows it.

"Did you order anything? You look like you could use it." Her cheeks go pink. She can't believe she said that either. She shakes her head, and when our eyes meet again, it's all business. "What exactly are you looking for, Finn?"

I know what she means, but my heart double-thumps anyway. "Promotion," I tell her. "My dad has almost single-handedly tanked Oliver Holdings' public image. I need to begin resurrecting that."

One dark brow raises. "You think you can do that as long as he has a Twitter account?"

"He's supposed to stay off."

She laughs. "And you think he's going to keep that promise?"

"No, but it's all I have."

"You have *way* more than that. I don't understand why you don't walk away. You're better than this, Finn. You always have been." She pauses, looking at me expectantly and I know I'm supposed to fill in the gaps.

Which of course I can't.

"My team drew up a contract for you," I say, reaching into my coat for it. "If you'd like to review it now, you can. Or if you want some time..."

Libby takes it, flipping the papers open and beginning to read. About two seconds later, she stiffens. "You drew up a contract with my company? Not with me?"

"Yes."

"How'd you know I had a company?"

"My attorney looked it up. This is normal. I promise I'm not stalking you." I'm just making sure if Maxon runs across the contract, he won't connect the dots, I think. My hands are getting sweaty, leaving ghost prints on the table.

Honestly, I'm pretty sure stalking would be better than admitting your father is out for revenge.

Libby scans through the pages, nodding to herself and not finding any unpleasant surprises—not that she would. It's standard stuff, mostly just agreements for photographs and video to be taken at her property. At the end, she shrugs and reaches for her purse.

"I have a pen."

"I brought my own," she says, not looking up. She signs her name, initials in two other places, and hands the pages back to me. Our fingers brush and sensation zings straight to my dick.

I swallow and my throat sticks. "You want anything before we go?"

Lightning-fast, her eyes drop to my mouth and then away. "No. Walk me out?"

"Love to." It's another slip-up, but Libby doesn't seem to notice. She keeps her attention focused on her scarf's tasseled ends while I leave payment and tip for my beer.

Outside, it's even colder than I expected. The temperature is dropping fast and we quicken our pace up the steps and onto the street. Libby's ancient Ford is parked next to my Audi and it pulls something in me. Things are so different now. Unlike in college, now I can afford pretty much anything she wants.

And she's driving a Ford from God-only-knows-when.

"Finn?"

I turn. Libby's looking at me and I can't tell if it's hate or...something else living in her eyes. She starts to say something and then stops herself. She walks around to the driver's door, opens it, and then shuts it.

Tell me, I want to say. But all that comes out is "Libs?"

The nickname wells up so quickly it's like it was waiting for me and she gasps.

"Don't call me that."

"Sorry." And I am sorry and I'm also...not. Because I think I do know what's living in her eyes right now. It's want—and I know it because it's tearing me apart.

I put both hands in my pockets so I don't reach for her and try to hold my ground when she takes one step...and then another in my direction.

Once upon a time, *I* kissed *her*.

This time? She kisses me.

CHAPTER 9 | Finn

And then she shoves me into the Ford. My back hits the door, her breasts hit my chest, and her mouth? She opens for me, melting into my arms not just like we've done this before, but like we never stopped.

"Libby," I breathe against the corner of her mouth. I'm not sure if it's a plea or a question, but she slants her mouth over mine again and I can't think of anything else.

My hands go to her face...her hair...her neck. My fingers tangle in the softness of her scarf and I tug it loose. An icy wind whips up between the buildings and she shrinks from it, pressing close to me.

And then I urge her closer.

We step deeper into the street's shadows, me curving down to meet her and Libby rising up to grab me. Her fingers dig into the collar of my coat and she hauls me to her, tongue seeking mine.

It forks heat straight to my dick. I go so hard I groan and I think—I'm pretty positive—Libby laughs a little as she pulls back, teasing me. She kisses the corner of my mouth, sucks my lower lip into her mouth, slides her hands over and over my chest until I'm burning alive.

"Kiss me harder," she mutters against my jaw.

It strings me even tighter. I spin us, putting her back to the truck and grinding my hips into hers. She sucks in a breath, feeling my hardness, and it makes me ache. I cup her jaw, tilting her open to me, and kiss her like she loves.

Like we both love.

As my tongue meets hers, her hands grip my waist then slide to my stomach...to my belt buckle. One hand fumbles unsuccessfully with the clasp while the other cups my hard-on through my jeans and I'm thrusting and thrusting before I even realize it.

"I love how you feel," she murmurs and then nips my lower lip, urging me on. My thoughts scramble. I barely register how the wind has picked up and we're outside and I should be freezing and she should be shivering, but then she squeezes my hard-on in her soft, hot hand and a groan escapes me.

"Touch me," she whispers.

Blood thumps into my dick. It almost hurts.

"Touch me," she whispers again and everything in me jerks toward her. One hand cups her breast, the other finds her ass and squeezes. She gasps, one leg sliding up mine and hooking tight against me. "Yesyesyes!"

It spurs me on. I thumb her breast, feeling her nipple peek through the soft fabric of her dress, and pinch it gently, pulling like she always loved. She arches into me with a sigh of pleasure.

"Missed that," she pants. "Missed it so much!"

So have I. She shimmies closer and I grip her ass tighter, spanning my fingers across her curves. Hitting the subtle outline of boning...and lace...and

Holy Christ, she's wearing lingerie.

I mean, technically, Libby's always worn lingerie. She likes it, likes the way it makes her feel, but I like it too. Maybe too much because now I want to drag her dress off and see what she's wearing.

I run my hands up and down her gorgeous body, feeling the outlines of silken things hidden underneath her dress, and nearly come on the spot. That's a bustier, I'm sure of it.

And thigh-high stockings.

With *garters*.

"My favorite set," Libby whispers into my ear.

I look up, and moonlight catches on her smirk, on the glint in her eyes. She knows exactly what I'm thinking right now and she's enjoying every second of it.

"It's black and silky and accentuates every curve," she adds, smirk and glint growing. She pauses, listening for anyone coming—the street's still deserted—and then says, "I look amazing in them."

She rubs me once for emphasis and I groan. "You look amazing in everything."

She laughs. "I do."

Which makes me laugh. Christ, I missed this—not just the heavy petting although that's mind-scramblingly good—but the laughs. The first time we slept together, it wavered from hilarious to comfortable to sexy as hell all in a moment. I've never had anything like it since.

Because no one else can ever measure up, I realize. She's perfect—and she *stayed* perfect because I didn't let Maxon hurt her.

"And speaking of amazing," Libby continues, stroking her thumb over the head of my dick. Even through my jeans, it's enough to make my eyes roll. "God, you feel good."

"So do you."

She feels like everything good in the world.

She feels like she's still yours, that voice in my head whispers. It rocks me to my core and I kiss her again. Hard. Just the way we both need it. Her mouth opens and I slide my tongue in, tasting her, enjoying her.

Libby gives to me even more and then grips my dick, matching me stroke for stroke. I tease her breasts, damn near groaning when they peak under my hands. They were always so sensitive. She needs me to kiss them, suck them, I'm sure of it.

In the distance, someone laughs as they leave the Hole In The Wall and pull back, panting. The world is spinning and then it re-centers and it's Libby.

It's always Libby.

Her eyes are so dilated, they're impossibly dark and huge. "I love you and I hate you," she whispers.

It cracks me in half.

Less than half. She's just blown me into pieces. If she knew what my dad had planned. If she knew what her father had done.

I swallow and...can't. My throat's funneled shut. She deserves explanations and I can't give them to her. I watch as two shadows cross the street and then we're alone again.

"I love you too," I say at last. Another truth. When it comes to Libby, I can't seem to help myself. "I always have."

Hurt and anger flare in her eyes. "Then why—you know what? I don't want to know. Not anymore."

They're the kind of words you say before putting someone away, but her hands are still all over me. I hold myself still, half-reeling from the pleasure of her touch and fighting myself not to touch her back. I'm not sure where the line is. I'm letting her dictate the rules.

Which you know she loves, that little voice inside my head says.

Which *isn't* why I'm doing it.

Her hands curl over my chest, but I don't touch her back. I don't deserve to. We shouldn't have done this. We shouldn't be *doing* this, but when it comes to Libby I can't help myself.

And she looks up at me like she knows.

"This thing between us..." she trails off, shaking her head even as her eyes go back to my mouth. She licks her lips and it damn near puts me on the ground. "This thing..."

I know. I know exactly what she means and if she can give me a minute—or twenty—I can tell her how I know. But right now I'm panting and she's panting and all of this is wrong, but my dick still goes hard when she says, "Undo your pants."

CHAPTER 10 | Libby

Finn draws back an inch, mouth hanging open. He's watching me like I'm half-wild which is probably accurate.

I *feel* half-wild.

Maybe more than half because when I walked into the bar and saw him waiting for me, it was like my body stood to attention. He looked broody and gorgeous and I thought I was immune, but the girls were right: Around Finn Oliver, I can't be trusted.

The way he stared at me when I walked across the bar made my skin burn. The way he's staring at me now makes me *melt*.

"Libs?" He turns my nickname rough, pooling heat low in my stomach

And now it's worse, I think as the heat spreads even lower. I want him.

I never stopped.

"Undo your pants," I repeat, taking a step toward him as I tug open the Ford's driver's door. Finn backs up and I angle around him, pushing him toward the wide bench seat. The backs of his thighs brush the edge and he stops, looking at me with agony in his eyes.

His mouth is already opening to tell me how we shouldn't and I don't want to hear it. I press my palm into his chest and he melts for me, sliding in and lying down. Without taking his eyes from me, he unbuckles his jeans and holds out his hands, inviting me on top.

I swallow, enjoying the sight. Beautiful, tortured, destructive Finn. Laurel was right. I can't be trusted where he's concerned. But he can't be trusted where I'm concerned either. I can *feel* his hard-on straining toward me. This attraction between us? It hasn't gone away. If anything, it's worse.

I'm already wet and needing.

Needing him, I realize. How can I want someone who has hurt me so much?

How can someone who has hurt me want me on top of him so quickly? Finn's fingers are dangerously fast with his buckle and zipper, but his eyes are all over me and I realize what I missed the most:

He looks at me like I'm the most perfect thing in the world.

But he left me, I remind myself.

But he wants me.

But he *left* me.

But I *want* him, I realize. He leans back a little, his hard-on straining upward in spite of the cold. God. It's mouth-watering and I remember how I'd wanted to suck him until he came, suck him until he saw stars.

It shouldn't be possible, but I go even wetter. I step up into the truck, slam the door behind me and pull up my dress to straddle him. It's too dark for Finn to appreciate my garter belt or thong, but it doesn't seem to stop him from muttering a stream of appreciative curse words.

"Christ, you're perfect," he whispers and it strokes down my spine.

"Am I?" I rise up onto my knees and then glide down, rubbing my clit against his length. He hisses in a breath.

So do I.

"So perfect. Do it again. Please."

"Begging already?" It's a joke from the first time we slept together and normally the memory would cut me to pieces, but now I'm loving it, loving him being at my mercy already. I rise up and come down and pleasure lights me up. I do it again and again, delighting in the feeling of my clit brushing his hardness through only a scrap of silk.

The moonlight catches on his smile, turning it silvery. "I think you're forgetting I can make you beg too," he says and his hands find my bare ass, taking control and urging me on. He presses me up and down against his hardness, teasing me and teasing me.

My head rolls back as I enjoy it, enjoy *him*. I needed this, I tell myself as Finn turns me boneless. That's all this is: need.

"I love you like this," he breathes and hooks his thumbs into my thong, rubbing it up and down against my hips until I'm desperate for it to be off.

No room for that maneuver, I realize. He's going to have to pull it to the side.

The idea—how quick and urgent and naughty it is—makes me soaked and desperate.

"Finn," I gasp.

And then his hands leave my ass and slide under my dress. He cups my breasts, playing with my nipples through the lace. I start to tell him the cups detach—and he finds out for himself. My bare breasts spill into his hands and he's rolling and pinching and teasing my nipples until I'm squirming on him.

"I need to come," I manage, thrusting wildly against him.

"Christ, yes. Condom?"

"What?" I blink, blink again, and my brain comes back to me. "Yeah."

I grope for my purse while Finn thumbs circles around my hips. It's my hips. They're not exactly sensitive, but under his touch? I can barely think. I stab my hand down around the floorboards. Not here. Not here. Here.

Thank God, I think, tearing into the interior pocket and finding the condom. I rip the packaging open as Finn's thumbs drift to my clit. He circles me once and I gasp then the clouds shift, throwing moonlight across him, and see his face.

And gasp again.

There's no denying the pure want riding his expression. If we were in my bed, I have no doubt I would be on my back and he would be licking me senseless right now. He used to ride me *hard*.

I loved it.

I push his hands away and roll the condom down, cupping his balls and enjoying how it makes him swear. "You are the hottest thing I have ever seen," he mutters.

And that? Only makes me wetter. I go to my knees again, yanking my thong to one side and coming down on the blunt heat of his erection. Even through the condom, he's scalding hot, and as I slide him inside me, I can feel him burning me up. It's perfect.

OhmyGod, he feels like everything good in the world. I slide firmly down his length, fitting all of him into me, and he hisses out a stream of curses.

Good, I think and then ride him harder.

But it only tortures us both. He's absolutely perfect and somehow not enough. I need more.

I want to be naked with his hands all over me. I want room to roll around. I want to drag this out and I need it to finish. I need him to make me *come*.

Like he did before.

I need him to block out everything.

Our breath has fogged up the windows and shadows have stolen across Finn again, but I can feel him watching me. His thumb goes to my clit while his other hand covers mine, pulling my thong firmly to one side.

Readying me.

My nipples begin to ache. Yesyesyes!

"Now," I pant. "Oh, God, give it to me!"

I grind down, reveling in his thickness, and he drags a lazy circle around my clit, making me moan. He's always loved making me wait for it. Always. And usually I loved it too, but now I'm desperate.

"Please!" I manage and even though I'm the one begging, he pushes me over like I ordered him. He rubs me again and again, spiraling me into a million pieces. Until I'm biting down screams.

Until I'm biting down his name.

CHAPTER 11 | Finn

Libby falls onto me, boneless and panting, and—shamelessly—I enjoy every second of it. Her weight. Her smell. The way she's still trembling ever so slightly, coming down on tremors from her orgasm.

She's blazing hot, sweating under her dress, and suddenly I realize I'm not any better. We've steamed up the whole truck cab and I'm panting like I ran a marathon.

Less work, more gym, I tell myself, willing my breathing to slow. It doesn't of course. I came so hard my head actually hurts, but I still want more.

When it comes to her you always do, I realize and take another breath, inhaling the smell of her shampoo and soap and knowing that this is all about to vanish in three...two...one...

Libby sits up and I wince, my battered dick still sensitive underneath her. She looks down at me, dark hair streaming around her shoulders. "Wow, I needed that."

I burst out laughing. That's a way better response than I was expecting.

A smile teases the corner of her mouth. "Put him away or I'm going to want him again."

My dick stirs and that promise of a smile spreads into a full-fledged grin. She shifts against me, stroking me once, and then gets up, slides over to the driver's seat, leaving me with a hard-on.

"I want to say I can't believe we did this," she continues, righting her dress, "but that's kind of ridiculous. This is *exactly* something we would do."

I shrug. "We have history."

"We do." Any amusement in her face drains away. She shifts and her whole body dips into shadows. "I wish you'd remembered that when you ghosted four years ago. You were my best friend."

"And you were mine."

"Don't. Don't start with that. If I really meant something to you, you wouldn't have done it."

I grind my teeth and say nothing. This was a mistake—for more reasons than just opening up old wounds. Seeing Libby now, I want tell her everything and absolutely nothing. I want to protect her, but I've already shattered her.

There's no coming back from this.

I concentrate on buckling my jeans and belt, feeling like a tool. "So what's this mean?"

To Libs' credit, she doesn't pretend to misunderstand. She focuses on smoothing her dress down and then says, "I don't know."

"Do you...do you want to see me again?"

Silence and then, "Yes."

We go quiet for another moment and then she turns to me. "So you love me? I'm supposed to believe that?"

I swallow. "It's true."

She studies me. "You know what the craziest thing about this is?"

"What?"

"I *do* know you love me." She looks me up and down. "Tell me the truth. I deserve it and you know it."

I open my mouth, close it. She's right. She's *absolutely* right. And yet I still can't bring myself to tell her. This is Libby's *dad*. She worships him. She has the kind of family I've always wanted. I can't destroy it.

For a second, I feel helpless and then I remember this didn't start with me. Her *father* was the one who embezzled from the company. At the end of the day, this is his fault. He should own it.

Or is that because you don't want to be the bad guy anymore? It's that little voice again and right now, it's cold and gleeful.

I take a deep breath. The truck cab smells like leather and fresh hay and I've spent enough time with Libby at her farm to usually find it relaxing, but now it just reminds me of everything the Brays stood to lose and James Bray—Libby's father—destroyed it anyway.

"Your dad was caught embezzling from Oliver Holdings," I say at last and my stomach sinks as her eyes go wide.

"What? What are you talking about? He would never. He would—" She holds up one hand and takes a deep breath. In anyone else, it would look like she was getting ready to lay into me with renewed force, but I know to wait. This is Libby trying to switch from emotions to logic. I get that.

I crack the passenger window and cold air snakes inside, clearing my head and the windows.

"How do you know?" she finally asks.

"Maxon found the discrepancies. It had been going on for years." I look at her and then wish I hadn't, watching her process that? It's like being punched. All the color drains from her face, and for a moment, neither of us says another word.

"And," she prompts me.

Fuck me, I think. "*And,*" I add, "there was a written confession from your dad—signed and everything. Maxon showed it to me."

Libby winces. She plays with the hem of her skirt for a beat and then whispers, "I still don't understand why you ghosted. Why does any of that, have to do with us?"

"It was a condition of our agreement." I clear my throat and look away. I'm not sure I can say the rest of this if I have to look her in the eyes. "Maxon was going to press charges—as many as he could get away with. You know what he's like."

Silence and then, "I do."

"So I made a bargain. I gave him what he wanted."

"You," she whispers.

Us, I want to say. I push the idea away. "Basically, I told him if he didn't pursue any legal action, I would go to work for the company. It was what he always wanted."

Libby nods to herself, staring at the clearing windshield. She's trembling a little and it kills me, but it would kill *her* if I tried to hold her right now, if I revealed to her that I'd noticed. Right now, I know she wants to appear on top of everything. "But I bet he wanted more," she says suddenly. She taps one finger against her lips, thinking it over. "You had to give me up, didn't you?"

"Yes." A single word and I still sound strangled.

She's tapping her finger against her lips again. "He didn't want his precious only son dating someone like me."

"It wasn't like that."

"How do you know?"

"Because with Maxon it's only about power. He knew I'd bail on him after college. You were leverage."

She blinks, eyes going bright with tears. "This can't be true! My father would never embezzle money. He's too honest. He's nothing like..." She clamps her lips together and grips the steering wheel like we're driving off a cliff.

"Nothing like Maxon?" I guess. "I'd agree with that. Your dad's always been a stand-up guy with me."

Which is true. In some ways, James Bray is a better father figure than my own father—or he was until I found out what he was really like.

Libby shakes herself. "Wait. Then how can you believe Maxon?

"Libs...your dad used *your* bank accounts. To hide what he was doing, he actually *involved* you. If I had let Maxon continue like he was continuing, he would've pressed charges against you and your dad. By cutting things off, I protected you both."

Color flares on her cheeks. "Oh. So I should be *thanking* you, huh?"

"No!" For about two seconds, I'm horrified—and then I'm pissed. "You've known me long enough to know I'd *never* expect that."

"Well, I never expected you to hit it and quit it, either!"

"I just *told* you the real reason I ghosted. You need to hear it again? Maxon required it. Again? Maxon. Required. It."

She pulls back like I slapped her, tears shining in her eyes. "I know he did! But I thought we were better than that!"

I pause, her words spinning through my head. Wait. That's not...It wouldn't have...

I don't know what to say and then suddenly I do: "Staying away from you was the worst thing I've ever had to do. It damn near killed me."

"Then you shouldn't have," she says softly—so softly it takes everything I have not to reach across the seat and hold her. "You could have come to me. You *should* have come to me. We were bigger than this, but you let us go."

For an entire moment, I'm struck speechless. She's right. She's fucking right. All this time I thought I was protecting her and really—

"Get out, Finn."

CHAPTER 12 | Libby

I need to think and I need space and I can't do or have either of those things with Finn sitting this close to me. I hold myself super still, but inside I feel like a landslide.

"Please get out," I say slowly.

"No." Finn crosses his arms and I can't tell if he's cold or settling in to be a stubborn ass. "Talk to me."

I open my mouth and realize I don't actually have anything *to* say. This is all too awful to even get my head around. Finn ghosted to protect me? My dad embezzled millions?

My dad involved *me* in embezzling millions?

"Why now?" I manage, hating how my voice is cracking. "Why tell me now?"

"Because I remembered—you reminded me—you deserve nothing less than the truth."

We're more than a foot apart, but the air crackles between us. It burns me up.

"And," he adds, "because I just realized I've spent four years blaming Maxon for destroying us when in reality? It was me."

I try to swallow. Can't. I hate the yearning in his voice. I hate the want.

I hate even more that I feel it too.

"Don't," I whisper. "Just don't!"

"Libby." He reaches for me and I slap his hand away.

"You're an asshole. Get! Out!"

This time, he does. He slides out of the truck and shuts the door carefully behind him. I want to drive off in a massive roar, stomp the gas hard enough to make the sickly Ford belch black smoke all over his perfect face, but I can't bring myself to move.

I stare at my darkened dashboard and wait for Finn's Audi to start up. It doesn't. One minute. Two minutes. Still nothing and then it hits me: He's waiting on me. He wants to make sure the Ford starts and I'm okay.

I hate him.

I love him.

I hate that I love him.

I crank the engine and the truck rumbles to life. I flip on my headlights and back out, maneuvering carefully around the other parked cars. Then I floor it, trying to get well enough ahead of Finn so I can pull over and freak out. Moments later, I turn down a side-street and park. Seconds after that, Finn drives past, missing me and heading home to Atlanta.

I turn the heater on full-blast and study my phone, debating who to call. My heart says Laurel because I can tell her everything and she'll forgive me and agree to keep it a secret and even put a positive spin on things.

But I don't need a positive spin. I need the truth.

Which means Ally.

Not that I'm going to tell her what Finn and I were just doing. I have some sense.

But not much, I think and hit her number. She picks up on the second ring, classical music raging in the background. "Hold on!" she shouts, and a second later, the music disappears. "Sorry. I'm writing a fight scene and I needed the ambiance. What's up?"

"I think I just found out something awful."

"What?"

In stops and starts, I tell her almost everything and Ally is completely amazing. She gives me time to collect my thoughts and let's me stumble around until I can finally say, "My dad embezzled millions from Oliver Holdings and he used my email accounts to hide some of what he was doing."

"I don't understand. That can't be possible, can it? You would've noticed if someone was accessing your account."

"It was during college. I was so focused on my studies I guess I...I don't know."

Ally pauses and I can hear the gears in her brain working overtime. She's trying to logic me out of this and there *is* no logic. At least none that I can see.

Another car drives past, its headlights almost blinding me and I wince. I need to get going, but I don't really know where I want to go. Home? I don't feel like I can look at my dad right now. Ally's? She'll want to keep talking and I think I'm about talked out. Laurel will want to know what's going on with me and a hotel's out of the question so that leaves...

No idea, I think, resisting the urge to bang my head into the steering wheel.

"Honey," Ally says at last. "I'm so sorry."

"I don't know what to do."

"What *can* you do?" Another pause. "Wait. How did you find all this out?"

I hesitate and then sigh. It's better to just be honest. "Finn."

Right on cue, Ally explodes, and while I listen to her rage, I notice she has a surprisingly great grasp on swearing—maybe even better than Finn. "How can you believe him?" she asks, finally running out of steam.

"It makes sense. I mean, it *doesn't*. I can't even picture my dad stealing a twenty let alone millions. But..."

"But?"

"But it makes sense when you start lining it up with his behavior and inability to get another job. In fact, the more I think about it..." I suck in a breath and blow it out. "Actually, I don't want to think about it."

"Fair enough. So what did you say when he told you?"

"That he was an asshole."

Ally snorts. "Well, normally I can't fault that observation, but in this case..."

"In this case, *I'm* the asshole. I shouldn't have said that. I was angry, but it's not an excuse."

"I don't understand. Why's Finn suddenly so noble?"

"We were going over the business plan and it came out."

"Uh huh."

"I'm not the only one who can't be trusted, Ally. The way he looks at me..." I trail off. I can't help it. My whole head is suddenly filled with the memory of how he swallowed as I approached, how tension radiated off him. He moved to touch me like it was muscle memory for him.

And I understood because I wanted to touch him too.

"You know what you have to do, right?"

Ally's question briefly disorients me and then I catch up, pushing away my thoughts of Finn. "Yeah, I know. I need to apologize."

"Sucks, but it's true."

"I still think he owes me an apology—more apologies, actually. Like four years' worth."

"No argument there, but you still need to step up. You've always been better than the rest of us about forgiving. It's probably why you and Finn get on so well. That guy has made loads of mistakes. He won't hold this one against you."

"Careful, Al, that almost sounds like a compliment."

"It does, doesn't it?" she asks, a laugh leaking into her voice. "Let's just say I'm mulling over the Finn situation."

"There *is* no Finn situation."

"Well, there's definitely the 'Let's make Oliver Holdings not look like jerks' situation."

"Yeah, there's that." Even with the heater going full-tilt, cold is still seeping under my clothes. I'm actually glad, means my fury and panic are wearing off. I can feel myself coming down and it's thanks to Ally. "I'm supposed to see him tomorrow," I add.

"Oh, good! Then you can get it out of the way and get this thing behind you."

"Definitely," I say and I even sound like I believe it. But this thing with Finn and me? I don't think it's something I can get behind me. It runs too deep. It's part of me.

And it's part of him.

CHAPTER 13 | Libby

The next morning, I get up even earlier than usual. There are the ponies to take care of and the barn to tidy up, and if Finn's here by nine, that means I'll need to shower and change and be back to the barn by 8:45 at the latest.

Which means, naturally, he shows up at 8:40.

I'm hustling down the stone path toward the barn when I see his car wind up our drive. He parks on the other side of my truck, making the Audi almost invisible from the house, and I slow, my heart squeezing and my breath rising in white puffs.

He did that on purpose, I think. In case my parents come back, he wants to make sure he stays out of sight. It's so thoughtful and so humble and so Finn, I don't really know what to say.

Or where to have myself.

He gets out, looking hotter than ever in a cashmere overcoat and dress pants. I've never had a thing for suits, but on Finn? I suddenly have an obsession.

"Hey," I say, walking toward him and tying up my hair. It's still wet from my shower and it'll never dry now, but I need something to do with my hands. I'm too scared I'll reach for him. "My parents will be in Atlanta for most of the day—doctors' appointments—you know how it is."

Only as soon as I say it, I flinch, remembering how Finn knows this stuff better than anyone. His mom died of cancer two years ago. It was after we'd stopped talking, but I had been there for all the chemo, all the radiation and consultations. Even if my parents are slowing down, I'm beyond lucky they're still healthy.

"I'm sorry I called you an asshole," I blurt. "I was completely out of line."

"You weren't. I deserved it."

"No! Finn!" I want to reach for him and I can't reach for him and I end up stuffing both hands into my jacket pockets. I take a deep breath and blow it out slowly. This is ridiculous. We're actually arguing over who should apologize. "No one should talk to you like that," I say at last.

The slightest bit of amusement lights up his eyes. "You always say stuff like that, but I never understand it. I *was* an asshole. You agreed. I should be the one apologizing."

I almost laugh. Almost. "Stop trying to logic this to death," I grumble, digging the toe of my boot into the gravel. "Just because you made a mistake doesn't make you...malicious. You made a choice. A crappy one, but a choice. I shouldn't have called you names."

"Wait. No names, but you *can* call my choices 'crappy'?" A smile tips up the corner of his mouth and butterflies twirl through my stomach.

"What can I say? I don't make the rules." It earns me a full-fledged grin and the twirling butterflies are suddenly joined by an embarrassed heat climbing up my throat. Why does he have to be so gorgeous? I mean, really.

"So," I say, shrugging. "Friends again?"

His eyes go bright. "Friends."

And then he offers me his hand. The same hand that has brushed hair away from my face. The same hand that cupped my ass the night before.

Among other things.

I force myself to take it, shake like this doesn't matter and I'm not shaking apart inside. "Where—" I clear my throat. "Where do you want to start?"

"With the ponies?"

I nod and turn toward the stables. None of the therapy ponies are inside right now. I have them turned out in their paddocks, enjoying the winter sunshine, but Finn will be able to see our set-up in better detail. Technically, if we'd waited a few more hours, he would've been able to see the kids coming for their sessions.

Probably should've waited, I think, chewing my thumbnail while he looks out over the paddocks. I don't know why I didn't.

Except I do.

My therapy sessions are deeply personal. I don't do this stuff because it's glamorous. I do it because it makes a difference. I'm not sure I'm ready for Finn to see me like that yet.

"I can't believe you've done all this," he says, turning in a circle to take everything in. I try to see it as he does and...fail. Thanks to the coming winter, the pastures are faded. Yeah, the ponies are shiny, but the fences around them are starting to sag.

Embarrassment prickles me. "What do you mean?"

"This is your dream, right? You've done it. I think that's amazing."

I stare at Finn and say nothing and the longer I stare at Finn and say nothing, the pinker his ears go.

"You've always been driven as hell," he explains. "But how many people know what they want to do in college and then do it? I didn't."

"I think you've done alright for yourself."

A half-shrug. His attention is trained on the arena we've set up at the bottom of the hill—or rather, what's *in* the arena. I wince. I really should've put those pool noodles and pink plastic buckets away. It looks like clutter and it's not.

"They're for the kids," I explain, stepping in front of him to block the view. I have no idea why. Finn has at *least* a foot on me. "We work on hand-eye coordination while they're riding. They pick things up, put them down. I know it looks like a junkyard, but—"

"It doesn't." He looks down at me and there's the tiniest bit of shyness in his expression. Every time our eyes meet, his skitter away. "Libs, I'm not here to judge you. In fact, if anyone should be judging, it's you. You're actually making a difference in the world. I'm...making money."

"Something I'm really happy to take from you." I'm grinning, trying for funny—and failing. Standing next to him like this, I feel scraped raw. We were so much to each other and now...

Finn clears his throat. "We can do all the photography and videoing here. I'll ask the crew to be as unobtrusive as possible. I don't want it to disrupt your sessions."

"Thank you."

A quick nod. "After we get the promo shots, I'd like to announce our contribution to the program at Oliver Holdings' holiday party."

"Fantastic." I fasten on the smile I use with the kids' parents, kicking into Professional Libby Mode. This is all so polite. We're being such grown-ups.

Why am I dying inside?

"I can ask someone in marketing to run the video clips together," he continues. "We could pair them with music—"

"Please, no Sarah McLachlan."

The tiniest smile. "God, no. We want people happy. Not crying."

We both go quiet as a chilly breeze picks up, whipping down the stable aisle. There's no need for me to ask if I'm invited to the party—I know I'm not and I'm okay with that. He's keeping me a secret, which is fine. I'm keeping him a secret too. We both want to handle this on our own terms.

Except 'my terms' seem to be my body going hot every time he's near.

And my brain remembering how he said he loved me.

"I always have," he'd said.

"Libs?" His eyes hunt my face and I have the scariest feeling that he's thinking the same thing I am. We're so close. How did we get so close? Did I move first? Or did he?

Or does it even matter because this thing between us is like gravity and we can't help but fall?

"Finn?" I swallow and take a deep, *deep* breath. "I want to try again."

CHAPTER 14 | Finn

"I want to try again," Libby says and the words slam into me so hard I nearly reel.

"You want to try...us again?" I manage.

She's fighting down a smile. She must know how this hit me. Who am I kidding? Of course, she knows. This is Libby.

And for a second, I don't trust myself to say anything because I know I'll say it wrong.

The wind whips down the stable aisle again and I step closer to her, blocking it. She hooks a strand of dark hair behind her ear and looks up at me. "Yes. I want to try us again."

My heart double-thumps. "Are you sure?"

"I think so."

Ouch. That's not exactly a glowing recommendation and I have to fight the urge to kiss her, to make her remember not only why we should try again, but why we were fucking perfect to start with. I fist both hands instead. "If you're not sure, I can wait."

Her eyes go bright. "So *you're* sure?"

I almost laugh. Caught. "Honestly, Libs...I've never been so sure of anything in my life."

Those bright eyes darken and my stomach pulls low. It was the truth, but also the wrong thing to say. For a moment, she studies the horses in the field below us.

"How can I believe that?" she whispers.

Yeah, how? I can't undo the past. I don't even know how I'm going to handle Maxon in the future.

Christ, I hope there's a future. She's offering me another chance at it. I cannot fuck it up—and maybe it's realizing the stone-cold truth of it that makes my brain start to scroll through everything working against us: my dad, her dad, the truth, the past, the fucking protestors. They're still camped outside my condo and probably will be for the foreseeable future. Thank God the guys in the van have stopped following me, but I keep catching myself looking around, checking everywhere for cameras.

"You'll have to let me prove how sure I am," I say at last and I dare to brush my fingertips along her hairline and cup my hand to her cheek.

"I want that," she breathes, leaning into my touch. "But I can't figure out the other part of it...your dad, my dad. Everything that's happened."

I hesitate. My instinct is to lie and say I have it all figured out, but I don't and I *know* she'll see through it. "I don't know yet. You'll have to trust me to figure that out."

Her lips part and I brace myself for some sort of retort that involves 'look how well you did that last time,' but she lets it go.

"I'll have to trust *us* to figure it out," she says.

"You're right."

"I know." She blinks up at me in a way that always, *always* makes me go hard. It's the perfect mix of cocky and teasing and confidence. "Maybe kissing me would help us get a few ideas?"

I grin, dipping my head so our mouths are only an inch apart. "Kissing you always gives me ideas: how I want you up against my bedroom wall...how I want you on top of me...how I want you in my shower and my bed..."

And my life. I start to say it and Libby rocks up on her toes and kisses me. Her mouth opens and I let myself explore: my tongue against hers, the line of her back against my palms. The kiss is light and sweet and then suddenly it's not.

Her fingers dig into my collar, urging me on, and I nudge her backward, pinning her against one of the stone pillars. Somewhere in the distance, a horse neighs and the wind dies down, leaving everything quiet except for Libby's sudden moan.

It rushes blood straight to my dick. I can't get enough of her—can't touch her enough, kiss her enough. My hands are all over her and I still feel like I'm desperate.

And she feels it too. Libby slides her hot palms under my coat and over my chest, exploring me.

Melting into me.

The morning is still a bit cold, but she's burning up. I can feel it through her sweater, her jeans. I've always loved how Libby dresses. It's always soft, slouchy sweaters and tight jeans, or snug riding breeches and arm-baring tank tops, but right now I hate it all. She has a body that was meant to be naked. Always.

She pulls back, her hair catching in the sunlight and turning her luminous. "This was always the easy part for us, wasn't it?" she pants.

I try to catch my breath—and fail. "Yeah."

"Do you think we can be more than this?"

"Of course." And I must sound so confident she doesn't push me. She pulls me down for another kiss and way, way too soon we're breaking apart.

"Gotta focus on work," she mutters, eyes still on my mouth. "That's the point of you being here, right?"

"Right." But the look that snakes between us is pure want, pure need. I clear my throat and then clear it again, trying to wrench my head back to the matter at hand. "Where should the camera crew park?"

***

An hour later, I'm leaving with the details on what we're going to do for the upcoming photo session and an agreement that we'll see each other in a few days.

But I have no idea what that's actually going to mean. How do you do Secretly Dating? I have no fucking clue.

Although, honestly? I'm glad we're trying it this way. Just thinking about what Laurel and Ally—hell, her *parents*—must think of me is vomit-inducing. There's literally no win here.

So. Dating, but secret.

I can do that.

Or can I? Because I'm suddenly wondering how to actually *date* Libby? If I want to move past apologies and show her why she should only want me, I need something huge, something I've never done before.

I merge onto the interstate and hit the gas. For some reason, driving has always helped me think, but it isn't helping much right now. Something I've never done before shouldn't be that hard. After all, when we were in college, I never had any money. My parents paid my tuition and I was grateful, but that was it. I crashed in company housing. Whatever money I had for living expenses I earned off app sales.

Libby was actually better off than I was, and when my dad threw me out of the company apartment, I crashed with her for months. I'd planned to repay her with the sale of my last app, but by then we weren't speaking. Everything I'd wanted to do for her, I couldn't.

But I could now.

I swing into the far-left lane and let the Audi out, flying past the other cars. It feels good to be in control.

Probably because everything else isn't, I think. I hate that. I want things locked down. I have a shot at Libby again. I'm never letting her go. I weave around a mini-van doing fifty in the fast lane and punch the gas even harder.

I could spoil her in all the ways I'd wanted to before. I mentally scroll through a few options and pretty much everything that would make Libby happy involves her farm and therapy program: fixing fencing, fixing the barn—all stuff I can do, but I damn sure wouldn't be able to keep it secret.

I scowl. Well, clearly that's not going to work. I need some other ideas. Something to work with—a jumping off point.

I reach for my dash, keying up the car's speaker system and speed-dialing him before I chicken out. This is humiliating, but Libby is beyond worth it.

It only rings once before Merrick picks up. "Hey."

"Hey. It's Finn." I pause. "What do you when you really want to wow a girl?"

CHAPTER 15 | Libby

So here's the deal: we're completely secret. He doesn't tell his coworkers or his family. I don't tell the girls or my family. We're going to see where this goes without everyone else weighing in.

Oh my *God*, how *much* they're going to weigh in. The prospect actually makes me tired. Or maybe it's just because I *am* tired. Finn left eleven hours ago and I've finally crawled into bed. I should already be asleep and instead I'm staring up at my ceiling and trying to muster up a more positive version of telling everyone who loves me that I'm back with Finn.

Hey, we're in love and we're going to give this another shot!

Yeah, nope.

Hey, he made a mistake and I forgave him so you should too!

That one almost makes me laugh. I can actually picture Ally's face if I told her something like that. She'd be furious.

And then she'd probably hit him with her car.

There isn't room for forgiveness here. There's only room for the truth—which means my dad's embezzling and Finn's cover-up will come to light. And when it does, it will destroy my mom.

It's already destroying me.

I roll onto my side and check the clock. Ugh. It's after midnight. I'm going to look like the walking dead tomorrow, but I still can't sleep. I grab my phone from the nightstand and open my Twitter app. It doesn't take long to find the most recent Tweets about Oliver Holdings and Maxon's rant. Part of me is kind of surprised there isn't more. We're only a week or so out from the original blow-up. Then again, with so many asshats out there, someone has probably done something just as bad—or worse—and the glaring spotlight on Oliver Holdings is starting to dim.

I wonder if Finn will break out agreement, I think. Technically, he doesn't need me anymore.

Only as soon as I consider the idea, I know it's ridiculous. Finn isn't like that. He's never been like that. He's honest to the core.

Just like my dad...right? I lie back down and close my eyes, but my head won't stop spinning and I can't stop trying to reconcile the man I know from the man Finn told me about. It just seems too...impossible.

My dad would never do something so dishonest.

Except he did.

I bury my head under my pillow. Being truthful about Finn or being truthful about my dad, either way I lose.

***

It's four more days before Finn and I see each other again. Mostly that's my fault. I have back-to-back therapy sessions plus farm work. It's enough to exhaust me—and it does—but I still find myself crawling into bed and wanting him.

I played with myself until I came last night and it still isn't enough to take the edge off. As I walk toward the Fox Theater, my nipples ache against the lace of my bralette. They're incredibly tender and yet I'm desperate for Finn's mouth to use them hard.

And when I round the corner and spot him ahead of me, waiting, that ache deepens.

He's in work clothes again—a dark gray suit with the jacket hanging open. One hand is fisted in his pocket and the other holds his phone. Whatever he sees on the screen seems to annoy him and when he looks up, meeting my eyes, my breath leaves me.

Broody has always been such a good look on you, I think, but then he smiles at me and I'm blown empty. No. Broody might be a good look, but that smile is amazing. Finn doesn't just look at me like I'm perfect.

He looks at me with such amazement, I start to feel perfect.

"I would have picked you up," he says, pocketing his phone without a second glance. "I didn't want you to deal with the cold."

I laugh. "It's November in Atlanta. After six months of summer, this is fantastic."

It is too. The sky is a robin's egg blue and the temps are hovering around sixty today. Of course, *because* this is November in Atlanta, if we wait five minutes the weather could change and go straight to miserable.

"Ready?" He's almost vibrating with tension and I'm confused.

"I don't understand," I say, looking around the deserted plaza. "No one's here."

"That's the point." And then he smiles and it's like the years of regrets and mistakes fall away. I'm not looking at twenty-five-year-old Finn, I'm looking at the Finn who's gotten every single birthday present exactly right since we were twelve. "C'mon," he says, sounding so confident...and yet his hand shakes a little when he holds it out to me.

I tuck my fingers into his and he pulls me to his chest, my face tilts up and he tilts down and then we're sharing the sweetest kiss.

I don't want it to end, I think, melting into him. We've kissed each other with want and in anger, but this? This is new.

This is perfect.

He pulls back a little, raining light kisses from the corner of my mouth to my jaw, and groans. "I can't keep my hands off you."

I grin. "I've noticed."

His hands slide to my ass and squeeze. Hard. "You love it too."

"Of course I do." I link my arm through his and he leads us inside. The Fox is probably one of my favorite places of all time, and any time I step inside, I feel like I've been swept into the stories from Arabian Nights. Everywhere you look, it's gorgeous Islamic and Egyptian architecture, vivid golds and startling blues.

It's also empty.

And I'm still confused, I think, turning to Finn. He won't look at me though. He walks us up the empty steps and into the equally empty auditorium. "Where do you want to sit? Lots of choices."

I laugh. "I still don't get this. What's going on?"

"I rented it so we could watch a movie."

My chest goes tight. "You *rented* the Fox?"

"You said it was your favorite."

"Yes, but not..." I take a breath. "You didn't have to do something this extravagant. If I gave you the idea that you had—"

"I wanted to. I couldn't afford the grand gesture stuff when we were in college. Now..." He does a small, half-shrug thing that used to mean embarrassment, but I suddenly can't tell anymore. We're on weird footing, different footing, and I'm not sure about it.

The lights go dark and the screen flickers to life. I settle back into my chair and Finn's arm slides around my shoulders and I get the sudden urge to giggle because this feels so tame in comparison to what we've done to each other in the past—and then Hudson gallops past and my long-ago laughter fills the theater.

My heart leaps into my throat and I lean forward, gripping the seat ahead of me. Up on the screen, Hudson wheels around and gallops toward the camera, playing. I remember this video. I took it maybe four months before he died and I'm opening my mouth to ask how Finn even managed to pull this off when Hudson vanishes and another clip appears:

There's me dancing with Ally and Laurel.

Then Hudson lying in his stall, snoring.

There's an entire minute of my parents waving to me from the grandstands of my last championship. They're waiting for my name to be called for the victory gallop and their smiles of pride are enough to make me cry.

I'm sure to the guy manning the film projector, this is the stupidest thing he's ever seen, but for me? It's absolutely amazing. This isn't just my life up there. It's everything and everyone who's important to me.

"How...how did...when...?" I can't even make sense and Finn grins.

"Remember when you had me move all those videos from your phone to your laptop?"

I don't—and then suddenly I do. In college, I was the worst about stuffing my phone full of pictures and videos and the overloaded memory always slowed down my phone. I had complained about and Finn had just quietly gone about fixing it, getting me a Google drive and moving everything to it. I'd gotten out of the shower one day and it was done.

"Your laptop was as full as your phone," he continues, "so I had to do the transfer from *your* phone to *my* laptop and then to the online drive. I ended up with copies. Awesome, right?"

I don't answer. I can't answer. My heart it still wedged into my throat.

"Libs? Is this okay?"

"You kept my videos all this time?" I manage at last. I'm trying to keep my tone light and missing it by miles. This means too much. "That's kind of creepy."

His ears go bright red. "Yeah, probably, but I couldn't delete your smile." He pauses and there's nothing but agony in his eyes when he says, "And I couldn't watch it either so I held onto it."

"For all these years," I whisper.

"For all these years." He won't look at me now and I'm actually glad. I can't name what's twisting through me right now. Is it shock? Bewilderment?

Love?

Because it feels like all of them. All at the same time.

"Well done." I make myself smile like he hasn't shattered me, like I'm in control and not falling for him even harder than I did all those years ago. "I bet you think you're getting laid," I tease.

"Only if you want to."

My pussy clenches. Of *course* I want to—and so does he. I can *feel* the heat rolling off him. But one of the amazing things about Finn is his ability to wait. One of the frustrating things too when he's making me wait, like for an orgasm.

My pussy clenches again.

I love it when he makes me wait.

"Finn," I breathe. "I want."

CHAPTER 16 | Libby

I don't know how Finn did it, but he got us a room at the St. Regis. The hotel is across the street from the Fox and all kinds of gorgeous. I've never been inside, but even the lobby exceeds the hype. Huge chandeliers blaze against the gathering winter dark and the dark stained floors gleam as we head for the elevators.

I'm actually a little nervous. Everything is so...fancy. It feels like stepping into a way more glamourous world than mine and yet here's Finn, walking through like he owns the place.

"What?" he asks, glancing at me and squeezing my hand. "Do I have something on my face?"

I laugh. "No. I was just thinking."

He grins. "You know how I feel about that." And as we wait for an elevator to arrive, he sweeps me into his arms for a kiss.

Moments before, we were hungry, desperate. Now...his mouth moves over mine so gently. He places both hands on either side of my face, holding me like I'm fragile.

Like this thing between us is fragile.

Which it is, I realize as the elevator dings and we break apart. This isn't just screwing in my truck. It feels like the start of something.

And whatever that something is makes me swallow as I step inside the elevator. I hold Finn's hand, leaning close to him, and feel my stomach pull lower and lower as we go higher and higher.

We finally get off, stepping into a hushed hallway. "Did you rent out all of this too?" I stage-whisper.

He doesn't look at me, but I spot how the corner of his mouth turns up—he speeds up too, taking longer strides.

"In a hurry?" I ask. "Somewhere to be?"

"Absolutely." And the look he gives me is so intense and so heated, I nearly trip.

He stops at the suite doors at the hallway's very end, slides in the key card, and then passes me ahead. The lights are dim and it takes my eyes a beat to adjust and then...

"Do you like it?" he asks, shyness edging into his tone and catching me off-guard. Finn might walk through like he owns the place. He might do multi-million-dollar deals. But when it comes to me, he's still cautious.

"It's gorgeous," I say and it's absolutely true. Everything is clean-lines and white linens, and through the gauze curtains, you can see the city lights like so many fallen stars.

"You're gorgeous."

I turn back, ready to tease him, and my words fall short. It's the way he's looking at me. It's the way I *feel* when he's looking at me. With any other guy, that would've been a throwaway line. With Finn, it's the real deal.

He suddenly palms his jacket, reaching for his phone. He glances at the screen and frowns.

"Work?" I ask.

"Merrick," he says, tossing the phone onto the bed. It skids across the coverlet and bounces to the floor. "He probably wants an update."

I wrinkle my nose. "On me? You wouldn't actually tell—"

"Fuck no." The intensity behind the words sucks the air from the room.

He doesn't just find you gorgeous, I realize, chest winding tight. He values you.

"What happens between us is only for us," he continues. "Merrick probably wants to know how you liked the Fox."

"Wait. It wasn't your idea?"

"The Fox wasn't. The movie definitely was." He's looking around and around the room, gaze going everywhere and nowhere. "I was stressed about our first date. I...I don't know how to be with you. Not anymore."

"What do you mean?" I ask and then suddenly I understand. We were friends, and briefly, we were lovers, and now we're...complicated.

"We're a Facebook relationship description," I blurt.

Finn laughs. Usually, that quiets any and all anxiety I'm having, but this time I only string tighter.

Which is stupid.

This is what I want, I remind myself. So why am I suddenly nervous?

"We're complicated," I finally explain. "Like, if someone asked me to describe what I'm in I would say 'it's complicated.' And I feel like that's insane because when I'm around you I don't feel complicated at all."

He nods. "I feel like I can relax."

"Yeah."

But right now, Finn doesn't look relaxed at all. He's watching me like I might bite—no, like I might *freak*. I love how he always gives me space to dictate how this will go, but right now I wish he'd kiss me hard, blot out all of my stupid worries.

And then I realize he might want the same thing from me.

"Are you nervous too?" I whisper.

"Always nervous with you." He rubs his thumb across my lower lip, and for a second, I find it impossible to believe that the man who can fuck me until I can't see straight can also be so incredibly tender. "I can't believe this is happening, that I'm getting a second chance."

"Me too," I whisper.

"Really?"

His breath hitches and the sound sweeps my nerves away. "Did you think of me while we were apart?"

"Every damn day."

"Did you touch yourself?"

For a second, surprise lights his eyes—and then desire darkens them. "Almost every damn day."

"Would you show me?"

He reaches for me eagerly and I step back. I wag one finger in his face. "Nope. No touching. Show me what you used to do. I want to see it."

Wry amusement turns the corner of his mouth up. "Okay, you're on. I'll show you exactly how I used myself, but..." he trails off, going to the bed and ripping all the pillows up from the top of the bed and tossing them to the middle.

"What are you doing?"

"If you're going to see how *I* used to touch myself, then I want to see *you* play out my fantasy."

Awareness prickles through me, pooling low in my core. "You fantasized about me?"

"Absolutely." And his gaze rakes across my clothes, undressing me. "I hope you're wearing next to nothing under there because I want to see it."

I grin. "Would I be wearing anything else?"

He groans, forking both hands through his hair. "You sure you want this? I can think of a million other ways I could satisfy you right now."

I let my hands go to my scarf, undoing it and casting it to the floor. "This *is* satisfying me. I love being in charge."

One dark brow rises. "*You're* in charge?"

The arrogant tone ripples through me and I go wet. "Well, of course," I say brightly. "Just look...you're hard already."

He palms his erection, eyes never swerving from mine. "You like me like this."

"Knowing it's for me? Absolutely."

"You're on," he says, dropping to the couch across from the bed. He watches me as he undoes his pants and his shaft breaks free. It's long and thick and hard. My mouth waters just looking at it.

"Oh, Libs? Since you're in charge, you might want to remember our agreement." He fists one hand around his hard-on and my nipples begin to ache. "Strip."

"Bastard." But I've already moved on to my sweater dress. I start to tug the hem up my thighs, teasing him, and Finn shakes his head, grinning. "I didn't say strip-tease. I said *strip*."

"Fine. Have no imagination." Then I tug the dress over my head and he hisses in a breath. "Now," I say, propping one hand on my cocked hip. "Aren't you sorry I didn't work you up to this?"

"Not at all." He sits back against the couch, stroking himself slowly. His smile is turning wicked.

And making me wet.

"In my fantasy," he continues, "you're desperate to get your clothes off because you need to come."

I suck in a breath.

"For me," he adds.

And now I understand. His fantasy was never about teasing himself. It was always about satisfying me.

Finn's wicked smile widens. "Up on the bed, legs spread."

CHAPTER 17 | Libby

"Up on the bed, legs spread." There's an authoritative tone to Finn's voice now, one that has me moving before I even realize it. My nipples ache as if he's kissed them and he looks at me like he knows.

Who's in charge now, I ask myself. How does he always know exactly how to play me?

I turn for the bed, making sure to give him a great look at my ass before climbing up the bottom of the bed. I take my time, partially because I want to torture him, but mostly because butterflies are pinwheeling through my stomach.

I sit down and take a deep breath to steady them. Can I do this? It feels so...bold. I've never touched myself in front of anyone and now I'm supposed to do it in front of *him?*

Until I *come?*

The idea makes my mouth go dry—even as my pussy throbs. I peek over my shoulder at Finn. His gaze is dark and intent and pinned to me. I can see how hard he is, how he's slowed his strokes. He's worried. Without me saying a word, he knows I'm nervous.

I flash him a smile, reach behind me and undo my flimsy white bra with one hand. His breath whooshes out of him and I turn around, kneeling for him.

"Fuck me," he whispers, voice gone hoarse.

Now I'm grinning too. Two can play at this game, and the realization makes me even wetter. I run my hands up my body and cup my bare breasts. His jaw drops.

And a second later, he recovers. "Lean back, legs spread."

I do, bracing both heels against the footboard as my back comes down against the pillows. They prop me up and I realize there's no where to hide. He doesn't just want me to play with myself until I come, he wants to watch my face as I do it.

My breath stalls. I've been naked in front of Finn, but until now, I've never felt this bare.

"Libs?"

It brings me back and I relax into the pillows. I watch his face as I run my fingertips along the edge of my damp panties and ask, "Did you fantasize about me like this?"

"Every time."

"Like this?" I run two fingertips over my already-sensitive clit and pleasure bolts through me. I'm desperate for a firmer touch, but it won't take much to set me off. The more Finn watches me, the more excited I'm getting.

"Cup your breasts for me again," he says, stroking himself from base to tip. It stalls me out entirely. I want to crawl to him, take him in my mouth.

"Libby?"

It's like he's speaking to me from a distance. I can't take my eyes from his perfect length. "What?"

"Play with your breasts like I would. *Now.*"

Again with the authoritative tone. It snaps me back to the moment and I groan, skimming my hands away from my aching clit and up to my equally aching nipples. I twist them like he would and my hips lift off the bed. I whimper.

"You're so fucking perfect, you know that?" Finn's words are barely above a growl. It's like they rub me from the inside out and I whimper again. I squeeze my nipples into peaks and my hips start rolling again, creating the tiniest—and most infuriating—touch against my clit as my silky panties rub back and forth.

"More," I pant. "Finn, I need more."

"Fuck yes you do."

My eyes fly open and I meet his heated gaze. Somehow I know I can't stop playing with myself, somehow I know he'll tease me worse if I do.

But even if I wanted to stop, I don't think I could. Watching him stroke himself? It makes my hands frantic. I'm squeezing and twisting and playing and it only gets better and better. Finn's staring at me like I'm slowly killing him—and I love it.

"Pull your panties to the side," he groans. "Let me see you."

Eagerly, I do and he swears, gripping himself harder. "You're soaked. I can *see* it." His voice catches and he clears his throat, clears it again. "Tease yourself. Do the circles I know you want."

God, how I do. One hand still holding my panties to the side, I use the other to palm myself, bringing two fingers up to circle my swollen clit. Pleasure turns me almost boneless. My knees fall wider apart and my head falls into the pillows. I'm vaguely aware that Finn's seeing everything—my emotions, my pleasure, my *everything*—but it only makes it better.

"I need to come."

"Not yet."

"But—"

"Not yet." He sounds half-choked, but there's a smile in his voice too. I peek at him through slitted eyes and he looks as frantic as I feel. His dark eyes are haunted and his jaw is clenched. He's using himself *hard*.

I want him, I think, feeling my lower lip turn into a pout. I *need* him. Maybe it's time to take control of this fantasy?

"I thought I was frantic to come," I remind him, forcing my hand away from my clit and dragging my thumb along my wet, *wet* entrance. "If I'm frantic, I'd already be screaming, right?"

Finn's eyes bulge and I know I have him. In his fantasy, I didn't wait for it. He's trying to tease me, make this last, and all I want is him.

Immediately.

Watching him, I slide one finger into me and bite down a moan. It's a double-edged sword, pushing me higher even as it pushes him, torturing me even as it tortures him. I need far more than this.

"Ah ah," he manages. "No."

"Yes!" It's one tiny word, but it comes out as a whine. I ease another finger inside me, delighting in the fullness. It's not perfect. Not yet.

I peek at Finn again and I grin. He's floored. I'll get what I want any second now. Any second now, he'll decide teasing is stupid when he could have me.

When I could have him.

I stroke myself, enjoying the friction, the stretching. "Why make me wait?"

"Because it makes it better for you."

A tiny fissure of alarm. Finn doesn't even sound like Finn. His voice has gone deeper, harder. Is he angry?

I peek again and what I see makes my nipples tighten even more. He's not angry. He's *close*.

"Fuck me," I say, rising up on one elbow. I stroke myself carefully, knowing it won't take much to push me over. While I had been nervous in the beginning about touching myself as he watched, now? Now I know I'm going to ask for this again and again. I love how it makes me frantic.

And I *really* love how it makes him wild.

"Fuck me," I repeat. "I want you."

He's up like a shot, jerking out of his clothes and striding toward me. I grin and start to push back—and Finn yanks me to the edge of the bed again. My heels dig into the footboard and I'm now so close to him, his hot, hard length rubs up and down my core.

"Can't deny you," he grates. "Can never deny you."

"Then make me *come*," I beg, writhing closer. "*Please*."

And I gasp when he enters me.

CHAPTER 18 | Finn

And when Libby looks up at me, I know what's coming. I can see it in how her eyes go bright. She's about to tease me back.

She's about to take control.

Libs licks her lower lip, and eyes still on me, slides one finger into her slick pussy, barely containing her moan. She's torturing both of us right now, pushing herself higher and closer. I love watching her come. Love it.

But this isn't how it's going to go.

"Ah ah," I manage through gritted teeth. "No."

"Yes!" It's half-gasp, half-whine, and she eases in another finger, stroking herself like *I* want to stroke her—and she knows it because she peeks at me again and grins.

Fuck, she excites me. I take a few deep breaths, trying to back down my hard-on. I'm on a knife's edge and she knows it, sliding her fingers back and forth and setting a pace I know way too well. "Why make me wait?"

"Because it makes it better for you," I grate.

Her eyes seem to go starry before she closes them, frantically stroking herself. I know we both love when I make her wait, but now I know something new: she loves getting me to the edge, getting me to that point where frustration and want are about to consume me.

"Fuck me," she murmurs, rising up on one elbow and slowing her pace. In my hand, my dick twitches. If she's slowing down, she's *close*.

She enjoys you watching, I realize, and bite down my groan.

"Fuck me." Her whisper is ragged. "I want you."

That's it. I can't take it. I sit up, yanking off my clothes as I stride toward her. She grins, delighted that she broke me, and starts scooting backward onto the bed.

She wants you on top, I think, damn near dropping the condom. It's sexy as hell how she takes control, but me being on top isn't happening. I want her on the edge of the bed, open for me.

I capture her ankle with one hand and jerk her to me. Libby's eyes go wide and bright with excitement. Her heels dig into the footboard just like I want and now she's open for me—so open I can run myself right up against her, feel how soaked she is.

"Can't deny you," I manage, balls aching with the need for release. "Can never deny you."

"Then make me *come.*" She wiggles closer, her heat damn near scalding me. "*Please.*"

And then she gasps when I enter her. I stroke her hard and her head rolls back, lifting her perfect tits into my chest. I love her in this position. So open for me. So bare.

I pull back and stroke Libby again. Her fingers release their death grip on my upper arms and she braces her hands behind her, letting her knees fall even wider apart. "Yesyesyes!"

"Never get tired of hearing that," I murmur, reaching between us and rubbing her sensitive clit. She arches into me, delighted, and I lighten my touch, grinning. "Say it again."

"Bastard," she moans. "I need this."

And it forks lightning across my skin.

"Please, Finn! I'm so close!" she whispers and it undoes me. My free hand goes to the back of her head, tangling in her hair and pulling her back for a more frantic kiss. She twirls her tongue across mine and stars burst behind my lids. She kisses just like she fucks: without any inhibitions, without ever slowing.

Can't deny her, I think, feeling how her pussy is growing even slicker around me. Her hips pump wildly against mine and I pull back from our kiss, run both hands down the gorgeous curve of her back until I cup her ass—and lift her to me.

"Finn!" Her legs tighten around my hips and her shoulders fall back and now I'm treated to my favorite sight in the world: Libby naked and open for me. I stroke her once, again. Her eyes close and her hands grip my forearms, egging me on.

As if I needed it. She's blazing hot now. So close. So very close. It will only take...

I pull her to me for one hard, *deep* stroke, rubbing myself against her clit in the way I know she loves, and it sends her over. Her pussy tightens around me as she arches off the bed, screaming my name.

I still want more. "Again," I order, grinding against her once more—and Libby rises to meet me. I push her over again, feel her somehow go boneless and tight against me and it's taking me too.

She drags me over the edge until all I can see is her.

Shaking, I lower us both to the bed, carefully pulling out and lying down next to her. I can barely catch my breath, and when I turn to Libby, I can see she's the same.

I lean my head against hers, kissing her cheek. "Never get enough of you."

And when she looks at me, I can tell she feels the same.

***

Libby

I lie awake long after Finn falls asleep. I feel like I'm soaring and I know it's the orgasm bliss—he used me perfectly—but it feels like something else too, like flying too close to the sun, like this is the roller coaster climb before the drop.

Like this is going to end horribly.

Just like it did last time, I think, fisting my hand in the billion-thread count sheets. Next to me, Finn stirs, pulling me closer and murmuring something under his breath. It kind of breaks my heart.

Even in sleep, he wants me next to him.

His arm tightens around my waist and I stroke the back of his hand. It's meant to soothe him—and it does, his face relaxes—but it soothes me too. I can feel my insides unwinding tick by tick. I didn't realize how tense I was until now.

Until Finn.

I run my fingertips along the smooth skin of his hand and then up his muscled forearm. It's so familiar and yet so new at the same time. I want to be the kind of girl who can just let things be what they are and go with the flow, but yeah, I can feel my brain winding up to obsess. This is too good to just let it burnout again. *We're* too good to let it burnout again.

I don't like admitting it, but the past four years has been like holding my breath. Laurel and Ally kept encouraging me to date and move on and be me—and I did. I grew my therapy program. I went out. I lived.

But I didn't date much. I just...couldn't. No one else could hold a candle to Finn.

"Then stop comparing them," Ally had said once, beyond frustrated after I'd cut another guy loose after only one date. "You need to get out there again. You can't get over Finn unless you go out with someone else."

"I'm not interested," I'd told her.

But that wasn't the truth, was it? I was still in love with the guy who'd walked on me and now he's back.

And now I know I'm in love with the guy who walked out on me to protect my dad. When this comes out...

Finn stirs again, sliding his warm palm up my stomach to cup my breast. It should be sexy—and it is—but it's mostly just comfortable and reassuring and I feel my eyes growing heavier.

Maybe we could just keep this a secret forever.

It actually seems like a good idea. After all, this is Finn. He's my pain and my healing and I don't how this is going to work, but I know it has to.

It has to.

CHAPTER 19 | Libby

I totally oversleep. Maybe it was the sex. Maybe it was all the worrying. But I crashed hard and when I woke up, sunlight was streaming through the hotel room's curtains.

And Finn is gone.

I sit up, stomach knotting. Something brushes my hand and I look down. There's a note lying on the bed next to me and I swallow, forcing myself to pick it up and read Finn's slanting handwriting:

Beautiful,

Killed me to leave you, but I had to go in to the office. Take your time today. I booked the hotel room for as long as you want it. Stay, enjoy. There's an open tab at the spa downstairs. Please do something for yourself. Massage, manicure, pedicure. Whatever you want.

Thinking of you today.

Love,

Finn

P.S. Every time I think of you, you're naked. It's starting to become a problem for me.

Okay, I think, rereading the note once more—and then again because the naked comment makes me smile. This is way better than what I was expecting. I dig myself out from under the covers and fish around in my bag until I find my phone.

Finn texted the same message to my cell.

And sent it to my email.

"A bit obsessive, dude," I mutter, but I'm still smiling. It shows how much it really did kill him to leave me. More importantly, it shows how much he understood how much the ghosting thing hurt me.

Progress, I think. Only as soon as I do, my phone pings with another text. It's my mom.

Where are you?

Late for feeding the horses for starters, I realize, guilt squeezing me as reality comes rushing back. Definitely no time for a spa trip. I'm in Atlanta and the horses should've been fed thirty minutes ago. I have farm chores after that and lessons starting at eleven. I'll make the lessons no problem, but it isn't like me to make my parents worry or make my horses anxious because their breakfast is late.

I kneel down and rummage through my cast-off clothes, texting my mom back with one hand.

Sorry. Crashed at Ally's. COMPLETELY overslept. There soon.

Seconds later, she responds:

Be careful coming home. Love you.

It's sweet and normal and I feel even worse now.

Which shouldn't even be possible, I think, tugging my dress over my head. I'm embarrassed to make the walk of shame out of here.

My phone pings again. Mom, I think, but it's Finn and I can feel my whole face light up.

Hi, Beautiful. Thinking of you.

I grin. I have about half a million things to do and right now, everything's going to have to wait a second. I text:

Thinking of me naked?

Seconds later:

Always. I can barely get up from my desk it makes me so hard. Someone's going to report me to HR.

I laugh, but before I can respond he calls me.

"Want me to send a car to take you home?" he asks. "We can pick up yours later."

If I weren't already sitting on the floor, I'd be there now. He's so thoughtful. "No thanks. I need to get going."

"Oh." Disappointment edges into his tone. "I was hoping you'd stay."

"Why were you planning to come back tonight?

"I could do that—we could do that."

And he just gets sweeter, I think, closing my eyes. "I have to get back. I'm really late."

"Shit. Sorry. I didn't mean for that to happen. You looked so peaceful, like you were finally getting to rest."

Because I was with you, I think and clap one hand over my mouth because now that I've thought it, I want to say it. This is all moving way too fast.

"No worries," I tell him, sliding my tights up my legs. It takes a bit of hopping around and I have to wedge my cell between my shoulder and ear. "You know...you don't have to do this stuff."

"What stuff?"

"Being extravagant. Taking care of me."

He pauses. "I didn't have the money to be extravagant with you before, but I've always tried to take care of you."

Just like I took care of him, I think. "It's just that the Fox...the hotel...the spa. It's amazing, but I don't want you to feel...obligated."

"I don't. I want to." Another pause. "I want to make you happy."

It's so simple and it cuts me straight to the bone. Even before we crashed and burned, Finn always put me first. Even *after* we crashed and burned, Finn put me first and protected me.

Do I really want to keep that hidden away from people?

***

In the end, I'm not even two hours late, but I still can't shake the guilt. It doesn't help that Sceptre is banging on the gate, glaring at me when I pull in, or that the ponies are whinnying like they're starving.

My youngest pony, Drama (because everyone needs 'a little drama' in their lives), pins her ears at me as I pass, the equine equivalent of being chewed out. "You're not dying," I tell them. Even so, I feel guilty.

Then again, everything makes me feel guilty these days so...

"Freak out later," I tell myself, pouring measured scoops of grain into feed buckets. "Work for now."

I'm almost done with everyone's breakfast when I hear the upstairs
apartment door swing shut. We used to have a live-in groom, but now
my dad uses it as an office, and when I hear labored steps on the wood-
en stairs, I know he's coming down to help me.

"Morning!" I grab two buckets with each hand and smile—even
though my chest tightens at the sight of him.

"Libby!" He limps down the last few steps, eyes on me. "I know
this is the part where I'm supposed to complain about you being out all
night, but I'm so glad you actually *went out*. What did you and Ally do?
How is she?"

This is the dad I know. The one who thinks I work too hard. The
one who asks after my friends. The one who actually likes my friends
and they like him too.

"It was okay," I say, my chest gone tight. "Dad...we have to talk."

He picks up on my tone immediately. Everything in him tenses.
"What's wrong?"

"I know. What you did. I know about it." I must have practiced saying that a thousand times on my way home and it still comes out broken. "I know about the embezzling."

He stares at me. "What about it?"

"You took millions from Oliver Holdings. Mr. Oliver could have
pressed charges. You could have gone to *jail*."

"Honey, there was embezzling going on and it came to light just before I left, but I had nothing to do with it."

"Finn said there was a signed confession!" The words slip out
quickly, unbidden, and I regret them immediately. My dad's eyes narrow.

"*Finn* said? Finn Oliver?"

I take a shaky breath, stalling for inspiration and coming up
with...well, none. There's absolutely nothing I can say that can turn this

around. Just get it all out in the open, I think and lift my chin, forcing myself to power through. "We reconnected a week or so ago and the truth came out. I wanted to know why he dropped me and, well, he told me this was the reason."

My dad's hands go from his pockets to the back of his head and back again. It's like he doesn't know where to have himself, but I can see the thoughts churning behind his eyes. Something's up—no, something's not right—and it makes my skin go cold.

"Dad?"

"And he said there was a signed confession?"

I nod. "Do you...not remember?"

He shoots me a wry look. "I may be old, Libs, but I'm not senile—not yet at least. I never signed a letter of resignation, let alone a confession." He shakes his head, lips pressing thin. "Finn's lying to you, honey."

"If he's lying then why did you leave?"

"Because Maxon pushed me out."

"How? You built that company with him. You—"

"Should have been more careful twenty years ago." He blows out a long sigh and takes a beat to adjust his sweater's sleeves. They were already smooth, but he smooths them again, and for the first time in my life, I realize my dad is embarrassed. Whatever he's about to tell me, upsets him.

"Maxon put up the capital for our company," he says at last, "and because of that investment, he wanted protection. His family's attorney drew up the contract and there was a small clause in it that said I could be terminated at any time and had no ownership stake in the company. I should have taken that more seriously. I didn't. I believed Maxon when he said it was just a formality, and for more than twenty years, it was. I treated that company like it was my own and it wasn't. I should have remembered that. I didn't."

My throat squeezes tight. "Oh, dad, I'm so sorry."

He waves one hand like it doesn't matter, but I can see it still hurts. Four years later, he winces like the memory stings. "I think that's the worst part. I should have remembered—I should have seen Maxon for what he was in the beginning and I didn't. I dragged you and your mother down with me."

"You didn't drag us anywhere."

Now, he looks at me and his eyes are haunted. "Didn't I? I promised you that therapy program and I didn't come through. You had to rely on an anonymous donation and now...now it's falling through."

I bite my lower lip. Now would be a great time to tell him it isn't falling through, but it's also a terrible time for telling him *why* it isn't falling through. It'll be a betrayal. He'll feel like even more of a failure.

But you still have to tell him the truth, I remind myself. Better he hear it from you than someone else. "Dad—"

"Can Finn get a copy of that confession?"

I blink, momentarily confused by the sudden turn. "I don't know. Why? Do you want to see it?"

He nods. "Absolutely, I do. I never wrote anything like that, Libs. If he says I did...well, I want to see it. Finn's always done whatever you've asked. Can you get it for me?"

I swallow. "I'll ask."

CHAPTER 20 | Finn

I gotta admit my first reaction when Libby asks if she can meet me at my place is to say no—not because I don't want to see her, but because I don't want her to see the protestors or, worse, the protestors to see her. It's a stupid worry. The building is huge and she could be headed inside for anything, but I can't shake the concern.

"You're quiet," she says and I tuck my cell a little closer, watching the door to my office. I was supposed to be in a team meeting five minutes ago and Merrick's going to come looking for me any second now.

"Not because I don't want you to come, Libs. It's...the situation outside. I still have some protestors and I don't want you to see it."

"I've seen pretty much everything that's been written online. I can't imagine it would be any worse."

There's amusement in her voice, but I still wince. This thing between us is fragile. I don't want to risk her seeing me in any light that might make her reconsider.

"Earth to Finn? You there?"

"Yeah. Yeah, I'm here." And I've already done the mental math. If Libby wants to come see me tonight, I'm not missing that opportunity. "I'll have the doorman let you in. Make yourself comfortable. Order something. I know I'll be late."

"And I'll be waiting."

Which is probably why the day drags on. I finally leave the office around ten, and even though my condo is maybe fifteen minutes away, it feels like a fucking eternity. I park in the underground lot to avoid the remaining twenty or thirty protestors and take the elevator up to my floor I unlock my door and the main floor is quiet, dark.

"Libs?"

"In here." Her voice floats in from bedroom and I practically trip over my own feet in my haste to get in there. Libby's curled up in my bed, under every blanket I have, watching television. The blue light turns her dark hair almost black.

She grins. "Hungry? I had sushi delivered."

"Starved," I say, shrugging out of my jacket. "But I can wait to eat."

That grin turns wicked. She rolls over, opening her arms, and I can't get to her fast enough. I climb up the bed until she's under me and then bend to kiss her. She tastes so sweet, like sugar and lemons, and when we break apart, I'm damn near undone.

"I saw the protestors," she whispers, running her hands up my back and loosening my shirt.

"Yeah."

"Less than I was expecting."

I almost smile. Leave it to Libby to make the whole thing feel funny. We pull my shirt off and her hands go to my belt buckle. "They're dwindling off," I manage, desperately trying to concentrate on our conversation rather than going brain-fuzzy from her touch. "Merrick thinks we can relax, but I disagree. We're not going back on our promises. Current plan moves ahead."

"To invest in the therapy program." Her hands slow, and for a second, I think there's something a bit off about her tone, but I can't put my finger on it.

"To invest in ourselves." I brush both thumbs across her cheekbones. She feels impossibly soft. "I want Oliver Holdings to be more than profits and losses. I want to give back, to make things better for people."

I probably sound like I should be standing on a soapbox and pounding my chest with both fists, but Libby smiles like she gets it. She probably does. After all, she's the one running a therapy program to help kids. She knows better than anyone about how broken the world is.

"I'm so glad you're here, Finn," she whispers, wrapping both arms around my neck and pulling me down for another kiss. It's perfect and nowhere near enough.

I pull back the covers, revealing a naked Libby. Her perfect breasts. Her perfect thighs. That *perfect* landing strip that leads me to my favorite place in the world.

"I couldn't wait," she whispers.

My gaze flicks to hers, holds. Does that mean...?

Without looking away, she takes my hand and guides it between her legs. She's slick and hot already.

Playing with herself, I realize, eyes damn near rolling back in my head. She's been playing with herself.

I rub the heel of my hand against her swollen clit and she moans, legs falling wider apart to enjoy my touch. I fucking love that. I watch her face as I play. "Please, Finn," she whispers and I know what she wants.

What we both want.

I lean to one side, groping around until I find my nightstand and the condoms. She rolls one onto me and every swear word I know escapes me. No one makes me feel like she does. Absolutely no one.

"Roll over," she whispers and I go to my back, Libby climbing on top of me. I want to enjoy the sight of her—gorgeous, naked, straddling me—but then she slides down my shaft with a hard thrust that makes both of us hiss. "So good," she whispers, rocking her hips up and down. "So so good."

And it is. She rides me fast and hard, coming within a few moments and I can't help but follow. I come in a black-out rush, Libby's name on my lips.

"Mmmm." She kisses my neck, my jaw. "You make me feel so sexy."

"You *are* sexy." I drag her down to me. "Unbelievably sexy."

She curls closer to me and my eyes drift closed. There is nothing better than naked, warm Libby lying next to me. I don't believe in heaven, but I do believe in this. Even so, something feels...off.

"You okay?" I whisper.

She stirs, hesitates. "I have a favor to ask."

"Good." I smile, drawing her closer. "I love it when you owe me."

"No, this is big, Finn. No joking around." She sits up, the sheets falling down to reveal the line of her spine. It's gone rigid.

"What's wrong?"

There's a beat of silence and then: "Can you get a copy of that confession my dad signed?"

"What?" I sit up and wrap one arm around her waist, pulling her close. "Why?"

"I spoke to my dad about it. We had a heart-to-heart about family stuff. He says there isn't a signed confession. He says you're lying."

Anger curls in my chest and I stamp it down. Now isn't the time. "I saw it."

"I know you did. I believe you." She peeks up at me through thick, dark lashes. With any other girl, it would be a ploy to get me to agree—and it works. I can already feel the yes forming on my lips. But with Libby, there's agony in her eyes. She can barely look at me. Her hands keep twisting the sheets into knots. "But my dad doesn't believe you and he wants to see a copy."

I smooth a strand of hair away from her cheek. "I don't understand what this will accomplish."

"I don't either."

I pause. "Is this what you want? Because I don't see any ending here that doesn't end up hurting you." It's true too. If I can get a copy, it will only prove her father's a liar as well as a thief.

And if I can't get a copy, I'll look like a liar.

Definitely getting a copy, I tell myself, hooking another strand of dark hair behind her ear. I don't want to give Libby a reason to doubt me ever again.

Of course, this means I'm about to give her a huge reason to hate her dad. He has to be bluffing. He doesn't think I can produce proof.

What if there isn't any proof? The idea hits me fast and hard and out of nowhere. I've known Maxon my entire life. What if this is another one of his lies?

Dread washes over me and I push it away, focus on Libby. She's tucked her knees under her chin and is hugging them close.

"I definitely want to see the confession," she says. "And I want him to see it too. Do you think you can get a copy?"

"Anything for you."

CHAPTER 21 | Finn

Of course the problem with this promise is I have no idea where to start. Where do you keep a confession of embezzlement? It isn't exactly something you throw in with an employee file.

Or is it?

My morning is packed with meetings and I can't stop by HR until around lunch. Thanks to my position, I have clearance to view almost anyone in the company. The trick is going to be making sure it doesn't get back to Maxon.

I scan my security badge on the 14th floor and the double doors unlock, letting me through. A couple of heads pop up, prairie-dog style, as I weave through the cubicles and whispers follow me. I can't really blame anyone for being suspicious. I don't think I've ever even been on this floor, and when executives come through unexpectedly, it often means someone is getting fired.

Hurry up, I tell myself, cutting past one of the breakrooms. No need to create anymore stir than you're already creating.

The HR teams are over on the southside of the floor, and as I approach, I spot Bev Jenkins, the HR director, headed my way. Statuesque and no-nonsense, she came to work for Oliver Holdings fresh out of Spellman College and blazed a trail straight up the corporate ladder. I've only been in a few meetings with her, but I've always come away impressed.

"Did you get lost?" she asks, smiling.

"Not quite." I hesitate, trying to decide where to begin. I don't know where her loyalties lie. Will she call Maxon as soon as I leave? Will she let it go? I don't know. The only thing I'm sure of is Libby and she wants this so...

"I'm sorry to interrupt your day, but I need to see the employee file on James Bray. Is that something you could help me with?"

"Certainly. If you want to borrow my computer, I can log you into our system and you can see it right away."

"That would be great. Thanks."

She nods and leads me through another few rows of cubicles. We reach her corner office—minimalist furniture, decent views of Centennial Park, and lots of pictures of her kids—and she rounds the desk to reach her computer. "Give me one moment to log-in," she says, long brown fingers flying over her computer's keyboard. "There. Here he is."

She steps aside, motioning for me to sit down. I do and quickly scroll through all the usual information—social security number, last known address, and such—and find a few scanned documents attached to his file.

The first is useless. It's a copy of the contract between Maxon and James, but the second? The second is pay dirt. I recognize the letterhead even before I scroll down to read the rest. Honestly, I should be thrilled, but my stomach is wadded up around my feet.

"How do I print this?" I ask.

"Like this." Bev leans across me, does another quick keystroke, and a small printer to my right hums to life. Seconds later, the confession spits out.

Good luck denying this, I think, checking the signature at the bottom. It says James Bray.

"Did you find what you need?" Bev asks. She's sitting across from the desk, looking through a file folder, and basically being the height of discretion. She's here for me if I need something. She's also politely giving me space. I grin. I'm being tactfully managed. No wonder the woman has been promoted again and again.

"Yeah, thanks," I tell her. "Is this system new? I don't remember it."

"Sort of. We fully implemented it a few years ago—when Carol left. She kept the majority of upper management employee files in her desk."

"Oh, yeah, I remember that." I'd actually forgotten about Carol Wright. She was Maxon's personal assistant for years and years. I close out of the second file and open the third. It's even more damning: four pages of photocopied Oliver Holdings' checks. They all have James Bray as the recipient and all have James Bray's signatures on the checks' backs.

I print that as well and close out of the employee system. "Thank you for your time, Bev." I push to my feet and pause, something prickling at the back of my skull. Only I can't quite figure out what it is.

And then a memory surfaces: We were at the company holiday party and Carol was laughing and talking to my mom about taking calligraphy classes.

"It's practically a job-requirement for me," she'd said, pride throwing her shoulders back. "Mr. Oliver is so busy. Sometimes I have to sign things for him and it has to look right."

I don't remember what my mom had said. Maybe nothing? I know I'd barely been paying attention. I'd been looking for Libby.

"I can do anyone's signature now," she'd added—but I still wasn't really listening. I'd spotted Libby and had turned away and hadn't given it a second thought.

Until now.

Because all of a sudden it's starting to feel dangerously relevant. Last night, I'd wondered if my dad had somehow set James up, if this was another one of Maxon's manipulations, but it seemed too far-fetched. How would Maxon pull something like this off?

And, maybe more importantly, why? He never does anything without a reason, however disgusting and selfish that reason might be.

Now I might not know the why, but I have an idea about the how: Carol.

"Everything okay?" Bev's concern yanks me back to the present and I realize how I must look: spaced-out and unprofessional. "Do you need anything else?"

"No, this is great. Thank you." I start to go and pause again. "But no one outside of HR has had access to them since the system implementation, correct?"

"Correct—wait. Do you have reason to believe someone *has?*"

"No no. Just...trying to connect a few dots."

"Of course. Let me know if you have any other questions."

It's all very pleasant and in control and I'm sure I look like my head isn't spinning as I walk back to the elevator bank. There's no way James will be able to deny any of this. It *has* to be his signature on all of this, but I don't feel vindicated and I'm not entirely sure I'm right. Not anymore.

I thump my fist against the down button and wait, taking a few deep breaths. It doesn't do any good. The more I think about what I'm about to walk into, the worse it gets. Am I about to bring evidence against my girlfriend's father? Or am I falling for one of Maxon's—and by extension Carol's—manipulations.

The elevator dings and the glossy metal doors open. I step inside, grateful the carriage is empty. I lean back against the wall and close my eyes. It's no good though. I see Libby's face in the dark. No matter what, this is going to gut her.

I'd sworn I'd never break her heart again, but as soon as the elevator reaches the lobby and the doors slide open, I'm headed for the parking lot and my car. It's James or me, and even though the man was the father I'd always wanted, I'll be damned if I lose Libby again.

CHAPTER 22 | Finn

I drop the confession and check copies onto the Audi's passenger seat and back out of the parking space. Probably faster than I should, but I can't seem to lighten my foot up. Our parking attendant—Dave—waves as I pass him then points to his watch.

"What gives?" he calls.

I grin. I don't blame him. Used to be, I never left the office before midnight. Now, I'm peeling out at six. Libby's changed everything.

Just hope this won't change it again, I think, glancing at the copies before turning out of the parking deck and onto the narrow Atlanta side street. As soon as I hit the interstate heading south, I speed-dial her.

"Hi."

One word and I melt. Christ, I have it bad. "Hi. How's your day?"

"Okay. One of my kids finally talked today. He dropped a saddle pad and said 'dammit.' I've decided it's a win anyway."

I grin. "Well, at least he's been paying attention to the talk around him."

"No kidding. His mom says it's practically her favorite word." She pauses. "So you've got the confession? Where are you now? It sounds like the car."

"Yeah, I'm on my way to see you." My stomach wads up again as I force myself to change subjects. "I got the confession copy for you and I got a copy of the cancelled checks. I'm bringing them by."

"Finn, I don't think that's wise. Let me meet you. We could go out to dinner—"

"I want to be there when you show him," I say, changing lanes.

"That's not a good idea."

"Yeah, it is. We're together, Libs. Even if you've kept that part a se-cret, he's eventually going to find out and I'd rather he find out from us."

"There's an 'us' now?" There's a smile in her voice and it kinda sorta breaks my heart. This is Libby: joking even when her world falls down.

"Hilarious," I say. "There's always been an 'us' even when there wasn't."

"Isn't that the truth?"

Silence falls between us and I concentrate on swapping lanes so I don't beg her to talk to me. I need to give her space.

And I don't want to.

Plus, the silence gives me more time to think—or rather, more time to remember. What if Carol was behind this somehow? What if she signed James's name? The idea that she could be deceitful enough to do something like that is insane.

But I can't stop wondering about it.

"So it's true," Libby says at last. "You're bringing proof my dad's a liar *and* a thief."

She sounds like she's forcing out the words, lining them up until they're perfectly straight and orderly. I hesitate. This is real and I'm usu-ally no good with real. I desperately want to tell her my doubts, but I want to see James's reaction for myself.

And I don't want to introduce hope if her father sees the confession and checks and spills everything.

"I know it's going to be rough," I add. "It's why I want to be there."

"I don't know that I want you to see that...see me."

"You've seen me at my worst."

A sigh barrels down the line. "I have."

"Then let me be with you." Silence stretches between us and I catch myself speeding faster. Seventy miles an hour...eighty. "Libs? Are you there?"

"Yeah. Sorry." Her voice has gone tight and I know she's crying and fighting it. "Will you be here soon?"

"On my way now."

***

Libby

I wait outside for Finn, sitting on the porch and watching my breath rise in pale puffs. Our gorgeous fall weather has taken a decided turn for winter, and even though I want to go back inside, I stay on our porch swing. Frost bite is worth a little bit of space.

Or you're just hiding, I tell myself. After all, when I told my dad Finn was on his way, we'd both looked at each and known what that meant.

"Good," he'd said finally. "I'll be ready."

Just as I'm convinced my toes are going to fall off—ridiculous, I know since we're only in the forties—the Audi purrs down the driveway and Finn parks on the other side of my truck like usual. When he gets out, my heart swings sky-high. Messy dark hair—like he's been running his hands through it. Closely-tailored suit—so I can appreciate every line of him. He's so gorgeous. And so kind.

And here to try to make this easier, I realize and I'm not sure if it's gratefulness or sadness that makes tears prick the corners of my eyes.

"Hi," I whisper as he comes up the steps.

"Hi." He leans down, kissing me softly, one hand cupping my cheek. His tongue teases me, setting that pace I always love. One breath. Two breaths. He starts to step back and I grab him, holding on tight. My heart's in my throat and I don't want to see what he's brought me, what he's about to prove about my dad.

But I have to.

Finn holds me close and kisses me harder and it's so good and so familiar—and yet so different. I'm kissing him like he's a lifeline. He's holding me like he'll never let me go.

His arms tighten around me, scooping me up to meet him, and come to him like I always do. This is our history. This is our dance. We know the steps by heart.

And after my very own forever, Finn pulls back. He keeps both hands on my arms until I'm steady and once I am, he offers me a slim folder.

"Figured you'd want to see it first."

He figured right. I flip it open. There are check copies on top. Each one made out to and signed by James Bray.

It's like the floor tilts under me. I almost think I'm going down. I hold the folder carefully, forcing myself to reread each check copy and each signature. Definitely my dad's handwriting. I turn the copy over and there's a letter underneath. At the top: From the desk of James T. Bray. At the end: his signature again.

I can barely manage the words in between. With every sentence, I feel sicker and sicker. He writes about how it had been going on for years, about how money had been placed in bank accounts in *my* name.

"You were right," I manage at last. Somewhere in the distance, one of the horses neighs and another answers. "I owe you another apology."

"You don't."

I do, but I don't have in me to argue. I reread the confession and then reread it again. I think I'm looking for loopholes.

And then I realize I'm looking for a fantasy. Even when confronted with the truth, I'm still searching for the father I thought I knew.

I take a shaky breath, suddenly beyond glad Finn wants to do this with me. He used to avoid conflict and now he's walking straight into it. Things really have changed, I think, looking up into his eyes. They're dark with concern and emotion. No, that's not quite right. They're dark with...

Love.

It nearly knocks me flat.

I'm in love with my childhood best friend and he's in love with me. I'm about to destroy my family and family was my everything.

"You sure you want to do this?" Finn whispers, hooking a strand of hair behind my ear. "It's your call."

"Not exactly. My dad asked for it. It's the whole reason you went to get copies."

"Doesn't mean you have to give in if it's going to destroy you. I want you to do what's right for you."

My vision blurs with tears. He always puts me first, which is more than my dad did by involving me in his embezzling.

"I'm okay," I tell Finn, sliding my shaking hand into his. "You ready?"

He nods.

And we walk inside to blow apart my life.

CHAPTER 23 | Finn

I follow Libby into the old farmhouse. Like the rest of the farm, it hasn't changed much since the days I used to stop by to pick her up—there's still the faint smell of orange-scented wood cleaner in the air and the pictures on the wall are all Libby riding or Libby with her parents or Libby with Tripp. It's a dizzying feeling of stepping into the past. We hang our coats on the vintage rack by the door and Libby leads me through to the kitchen.

Her mom's sitting at the table, tension making her practically vibrate. She swallows before saying, "Hello, Finn. It's been a long time."

"It has, Mrs. Bray. I'm sorry we had to reconnect over...this."

Everyone's eyes slide to the folder in Libby's hand and Mrs. Bray inhales hard, like she's trying not to cry.

Fuck me. If she cries, I will have zero clue what to do about it. Mrs. Bray has always been like a second mom to me—and a best friend to Libby. I can look at her and see what Libs will look like in another twenty years: still beautiful, but a bit more lined, a bit curvier.

Far more stressed, I realize and suddenly hope I can keep Libby from ever feeling what her mother has gone through over the past years.

There's movement to my right and a figure shuffles into the kitchen. James. He's thinner than he was and his shoulders are a little more stooped. Leaving Oliver Holdings should've been a weight off him, but he looks ancient.

"Sweetheart," he says to his wife, pointedly ignoring me as he limps past me. He looks at Libby. She looks back and then silently passes him the folder. He opens it, and for several moments, there's only the sound of the ticking grandfather clock and the wind battering the side of the house.

Finally, he clears his throat and closes the folder. "I didn't write this." He passes everything back to Libby, still ignoring me. I'm actually glad. It gives me a chance to really study him and what I see? It turns my whole body to ice. James isn't lying.

Which means there's a hell of a lot more to this.

"I have no idea where this came from," he says to Libby.

She blinks. "But that's your signature."

"It can't be."

"Dad..." They glare at each other.

"May I see?" Mrs. Bray asks. Without breaking her stare-down, Libby passes her mother the folder. "She's right, dear," Mrs. Bray says, glancing over the contents. "That *is* your handwriting."

"What if it isn't?" I ask, leaning back against the countertop.

Libby slowly turns to me. "What?"

"What if it isn't his signature? What if it's a forgery?"

Libby's head tilts. She's staring at me like I've just suggested Santa Claus is real. "This isn't a soap opera. Who would do something like that?"

I bite my lower lip. Someone who was so desperate to please Maxon she would be willing to do anything. "Do you remember Carol Wright?" I ask James.

The older man pauses, studying me. "Of course, I do."

"I remember a comment she made once—something about how she used to sign for my father and some of the other stakeholders. She even took a class to improve her technique."

A bitter smile. "Are you suggesting this because you think it's true or because you're trying to trap me into saying something to make the situation worse?"

"Because I'm wondering if it is true. It certainly seems...possible." And the longer James meets my eyes without looking away, without any semblance of embarrassment, the more I begin to think it's more than possible. It's true.

James turns back to Libby. "I thought you knew me better than this. I thought you loved me—"

"I do! But look what it says!"

"Yes, look! Are those even your accounts?"

Libby falters. She glances down at the cancelled checks and bites her lower lip. "I don't recognize them, but—"

"But you think I would involve you in something illegal?" His voice has gone tight with fury and hurt.

And it hits Libby full-on. Just like I knew it would.

Her mouth parts like he slapped her and then she pulls herself together, shakes herself a little. "What am I supposed to think? This looks like your signature and you didn't tell me the real reason you left Oliver Holdings until yesterday!"

"Because it had nothing to do with you!" he yells. "This was between me"—his gaze cuts to me and it's filled with pure hatred—"and the two of them."

I start to say I didn't have a fucking hand in any of this, but James stops me.

"You were like a son to me," he spits, turning away. "You were family!"

He stalks from the kitchen, leaving the rest of us behind. Mrs. Bray begins to cry quietly, but Libby doesn't move—one look at her face though and I can tell she's shattered.

***

Libby

I suck in a breath and then another. Dad isn't interested in anything else Finn has to say, and when my mom's eyes meet mine across the kitchen, I know it's time to leave. Thing is...they're expecting me to stay and all I want to do right now is go with Finn, go back to Atlanta, disappear into his practically empty condo.

And pretend this isn't happening.

"I need a minute," I tell my mother and then bolt from the kitchen before she can respond. Finn's hot on my heels and we head back outside, tugging on our coats.

I walk him to his car and Finn cuts ahead of me. He leans back against the Audi's glossy door and pulls me to him, tucking his coat around me. At any other time, my pulse would slow and my brain would go fuzzy, but I can't shake what just happened.

"There's only one way to finish this," Finn murmurs against my hair.

"What's that? By burning down our house? Because that would definitely finish it." I mean it as a joke, but it his way too close to bone. The way my father had looked at me back there? I'd nearly cried. He's acting like I betrayed him, like I'm choosing sides and I'm not.

Finn rubs his chin against the top of my head. "Let's go talk to Carol."

"What?"

"Let's go see her. I can find out where she lives. She would still be on the Oliver Holdings mailing list."

I hesitate. This seems like a terrible idea and yet... "Okay."

"Good." He opens the Audi's door and the smell of leather and new car wafts out. "After you."

I hesitate again. Do I really want to do this?

Can I not?

I get in and Finn closes the door. He walks around the car and slides behind the wheel, turning to me as he reverses us out of the driveway. "We'll find this out together, right?"

"Yeah." I smile. "Together."

***

The cottages on this side of town are a little run-down and a little funky. Some are bright pink. Some are teal. Some have tarps over their roofs thanks to the recent bout of storms. It isn't where I would've thought a personal assistant like Carol would've ended up.

Finn checks his phone once more and slows down, looking toward a tidy white cottage on our right. "This should be it."

We turn in and park next to a small sedan. As I undo my seat belt, the curtains twitch and a moon pale face appears at the window.

"I think she's home," I whisper.

Finn glances up and the face disappears. "Not promising."

"Yeah."

We get out and walk up the stone path to the front porch. It needs a coat of paint, the pale blue ceiling is peeling, and there's pollen from seasons past collected in the all the porch's corners.

I pull my coat a little tighter against me and Finn takes my hand, squeezing it. "Whatever happens, it'll be okay."

"Easy for you to say."

He starts to respond and something metal scrapes. A lock, I realize as the door swings open. Carol Wright appears behind the screen door.

She looks from Finn to me and sighs. "I knew you'd come one day."

CHAPTER 24 | Libby

Everything about Carol's house is overstuffed. From the glass figurines crowding almost every flat space to the oversized furniture crammed into the cottage's tiny spaces, I almost don't know where to look first.

Much less sit.

She motions toward a floral-patterned couch piled high with pillows and when I hesitate, she bats a few of them onto the floor. "Just make yourself comfortable, honey. We don't stand on ceremony around here."

I nod, sitting down and feeling crazy out of place even though Finn takes the chair next to me. It isn't just the situation—well, not entirely—it's the way Carol looks at him, like they have history and she's missed him.

Did they? I wonder. I don't remember much about Carol, but even my few memories barely match her now. The curvy pin-up worthy figure is hidden under a fraying housecoat and her hair is shot through with gray.

"It's so nice to see you, Finn," she says, sitting down across from us. "You're even more handsome now. I can really see your father in you now."

Oof. I try not to wince. Starting off with Maxon is so not a good way to get things started.

"Thank you," Finn says. "You remember James Bray's daughter, Libby, right?"

A ghost of a scowl crosses her face. It goes so quickly I almost miss it. "Of course."

Two words and yet they feel loaded. She looks at me, smiling like she's been fed secrets, and I suddenly wonder what I've walked into.

She turns her attention back to Finn. "How's Maxon?"

"He's Maxon." Finn pairs it with a bland smile, but I can see how the muscles in his jaw jump. "Actually, I wanted to ask you a few things about when you worked for him."

She nods, smoothing and re-smoothing her housecoat over her knees. She won't meet his eyes and the base of my spine begins to knot. Something's not quite right here.

And when Finn tenses, I know he knows it too.

"I know my father valued your input greatly," he begins, bracing his elbows on his knees and leaning forward a little. The movement attracts her attention and she looks up at him, something hungry in her eyes. "You were involved in many of the day-to-day operations, weren't you?"

"I was." Her chin lifts. "I didn't finish college, but he knew street smarts when he saw them. I went from answering his phones to supporting him in every way."

Did she mean for that to sound so...suggestive? Finn's right hand flexes briefly into a fist and then he shakes it loose. "You supported a lot of the upper management though too, didn't you?" he continues lightly. "You worked with James Bray from time to time."

Carol's eyes cut to me and she squirms. "Only when absolutely necessary. He had his own team."

"The team who helped him embezzle a few million, right?"

Another squirm. Her eyes dart to me. "That's what I was told."

"Is that what you believe?" The question skids out of me and I don't even regret it. "You really believe he was capable of something like that?"

For a second, I think I've ruined everything. For a second, I know I've ruined everything because she stares me down like I'm disgusting. Silence stretches between us, thick and heavy.

"No," she says at last. "I don't think he's capable of it. Not anymore."

My pulse begins to pound. "What do you mean?"

She shifts in her armchair, playing with the tasseled edge of one of her pillows. "Maxon showed me the list of deposits and he said they'd been tracked back to James. I was horrified. I mean, can you imagine?"

She looks to both of us and when we say nothing, she shrugs, continues: "Maxon told me James had been caught red-handed, but it was such a fraught situation, we should type up a confession and have him sign it. It would be easier that way. It would keep emotion out of it. We would stick to the facts and then James would sign it."

"And that's what happened?"

She nods. "Maxon told me what to type and left for the evening. It wasn't until much later that he called me and said James wouldn't sign."

"Because it wasn't true!"

Finn puts one hand on my knee, rubbing my jeans. With anyone else, it would make me even angrier. With Finn, it somehow makes my anger stand down a bit.

But only a bit.

Carol watches us closely, her eyes going from Finn's hand to my face. She makes a tsk-ing noise.

"Then what happened?" Finn prompted.

Her chin lifts a little higher this time. "Maxon said James wouldn't sign and we would have to do it for him. He asked if I could do it, if he could come by that night."

"He met you...here."

"Yes."

A charged look snakes between them and, finally, a piece falls into place for me: she was sleeping with Maxon. She had to be.

Carol inhales hard through her nose, like she's fighting off tears and says, "So I did it. I signed James's name. It was easy. I had taken a calligraphy class a few years before to perfect my handwriting and I often signed for many of the upper level managers. It was expected."

"And it never occurred to you that this was wrong?"

"He told me it happened. I believed him. It was only after that..." She shakes her head and glances around the room. "It was only afterward that I realized something wasn't right and I started investigating. Here. Look."

She stands, rubbing shaking hands down her housecoat, and shuffles to a desk mostly hidden behind another loveseat. "I made copies of everything," she says, opening a drawer.

What? Finn and I exchange a quick look before she turns around, file folders in hand. They're wrist-thick with paperwork.

"Deposits were being made," she continues. "The money was definitely going out, but I don't recognize the accounts. I was told they were yours." She gives me a questioning look and I stare back defiantly.

"They're not mine."

Finn takes the paperwork and flips through it, pausing here and there to read. Whatever he sees makes his mouth tighten. "Thank you for showing us this," he says at last. "Could I take it?"

"Of course! Of course!" Carol hesitates. "I hope you know how much I loved your father. I really did—" She reaches for him and Finn pulls back.

"You knew he was married," he says quietly.

"But he told me she was awful." Her eyes have gone faraway. She might be with us, but she's remembering some old moment and it makes her look a heartbeat away from tears. "He told me he loved me, that he hadn't felt this way *ever* with her." She fists both hands, burying them in her lap, and looks at Finn. "You were always such a nice young man. I know you had your differences with your father, but I thought you would come around."

"There's no coming around with Maxon," Finn says. "You're either under his thumb or you're out."

"Yes, yes. I realize that now. But at the time...at the time, I thought things could be different with us. I thought *I* was different."

And then she found out she'd been used. My heart aches even as my anger continues to simmer. This was a woman who would do anything for those she loved.

Even destroy my father.

What a horrible thing to have done and what a horrible thing to have to live with.

"I really did think we were going to do things right. We were going to get married. I bought all the furniture we were supposed to need." She gestures to the room around us. "It wasn't supposed to be like this. I'm not that kind of person."

"Except you are." Finn's expression has hardened and I know he isn't thinking about my dad. He's thinking about his mom and all the infidelities she endured from Maxon. She would've been struggling through her last chemo session while this was going on. How horrible.

"Why are you telling us all of this?" I manage, throat squeezing. "Why not come forward before?"

"I'm afraid and I'm ashamed and I knew...I knew it would eventually come around, but I didn't know when. I thought I could live with it, but when I saw you pull up..."

We wait while she does another sharp inhale, but it does nothing for the tears. They slide down her cheeks, one after another. "When I saw you pull up, I knew I couldn't live with it anymore. I could have lied. You would never have known. I hope you remember that when you think of me—and I hope you remember to tell the authorities."

"Wait. You think he's pressing charges?" I'm floored and then I'm not. This is fraud, right? And embezzlement and forgery and...I'm not sure of anything else. My only experience with the law is a few speeding tickets and a bunch of CSI: Miami.

"I could," Finn says slowly. "I could bring all of this to light."

She nods. "And I would deserve it. If I go to jail"—her voice wavers—"I deserve it. I'm done hiding. You have the truth. Now you can decide what to do with it."

CHAPTER 25 | Libby

Outside, the weather is turning cold and there are storm clouds rolling in from the west. Nothing like some freezing rain, I think, scowling. I follow Finn to the car and he opens the door for me, shuts it behind me, and says nothing when he climbs back behind the wheel.

"How—"

"One second."

"What—" And then I realize what's going on: Finn's fighting himself off the edge. He starts the car and pulls us out of the driveway, hands gone white-knuckled around the steering wheel. Minutes later, he sees a gas station and pulls in. We park next to souped-up Honda and Finn stares through the windshield, watching people walk past us like he's never seen anything like them.

"I don't even know what to say," he manages at last, voice shaking.

Still on the edge, I realize and shift a little closer. I don't know if I should touch him or not, talk or not. I remember these moments from years ago, but I suddenly doubt my ability to handle them.

"How did I not see this?" he manages through gritted teeth. "Why didn't I question him? Why?"

I touch his arm and he doesn't even notice. His breath is coming hard and his focus is narrowing, turning inward. He might be with me, but he's not *with* me. He's reliving those moments with Maxon four years ago.

With my dad this afternoon.

"Finn," I whisper. "Come back to me? Please? Come back to me. It's done. It's over. I'm here." His head pulls back an inch. It's barely anything, but now I know he heard me. "Finn, I'm here," I repeat.

And he turns, blinks at me like he's suddenly realizing this. His breath is jagged and his eyes are stark, but he *turned* to me. This is huge and I can't stop my smile. This is Finn trying to bring himself back.

To me.

"I love you," I say, the words breaking my heart even as they fill it. "I love you. Come back."

"You can't love me."

"But I do."

"I destroy everything I love." His voice sounds rusted, like he dredged it up from some part of himself he left in the rain to rot. "Everything."

"You don't. You had no way of knowing this was all a lie."

He jerks his head to one side, starting to deny it, and then stops. He studies my face for a moment and then another. "You're right," he says at last.

But I can tell he doesn't believe a word of it.

***

We sit for a long time in silence. After what we just learned, the quiet should feel oppressive, but it's not. I'm not happy, but sitting next to Finn makes me feel slightly more in control, a little more capable of handling everything that's about to come our way.

Between our two seats, my cell begins to vibrate. Incoming call. Ally. "You want to get that?" Finn asks, gaze focused straight ahead again. "I can stand outside if you want a minute."

"No! No way am I making you stand in the cold!" I send the call the call to voicemail. Even if I were alone, I probably wouldn't have picked up. I don't know what to say right now. I'm too drained and Ally would want explanations and honestly...I don't think I fully understand all of this enough *to* explain it.

Or maybe I just don't want to. What Carol did is awful—beyond awful—but she's paying for it now.

For a minute, Finn and I watch customers walk in and out of the gas station. Everyone is bundled up and glancing at the sky. It looks like it's about to open up and pour any second now. I shiver and feel Finn's gaze go to me.

And stick.

Fury rolls off him in waves. Not at me, I know that, but it still makes me uneasy. Angry Finn has been known to do some incredibly stupid shit.

"Are you cold?" he asks. "I can turn the heat up."

I shake my head. "I'm okay. Just...in shock, I guess."

His hand goes to my knee, rubbing relaxing circles. "I get that."

Yeah, I think. You probably do.

For him, this is more than finding out Carol deliberately forged my dad's signatures. It's discovering another affair his father had while being married to his mother. It's discovering a new level of deceit from Maxon. Maybe even realizing if his dad was capable of something like this, what else has he done?

What else will he do?

Because Finn thinks about all that stuff. Today will torment him and I wish I could protect him from that.

I put my hand over Finn's, running my thumb up and down the backs of his long fingers. "I still don't understand why either of them would resort to forging a false confession. If he wanted my dad out at any point, he could have just fired him—which he did. There was that clause in their original contract. There was no need to fabricate anything."

Finn stiffens and pulls away. "If I had to guess...Maxon's keeping the confession as a get-out-of-jail-free card."

"What?"

"Those cashed checks? They were real. Money did go out, but like Carol said, we don't know where it went. What if Maxon was framing your dad?"

I can feel the blood drain from my face. I turn in my seat to face Finn. Our breath is fogging up the windows, blurring the parking lot and gas station outside. "But that means if it ever comes out...my dad could get in trouble for all of this."

"Exactly." He's back to picking at the Audi's steering wheel again, eyes unfocused and faraway. "Maxon created a cover. If he was smart enough to hide the bank accounts—which he is—no one would be able to trace it back to him. Your dad would take the fall."

"And you think he's still planning for that?"

A shrug. "Hard to tell. With Maxon, anything's possible."

For a second, I think I'm going to be sick. I feel like there's a ticking time bomb sitting next to us. My family could be safe for another ten years or another ten minutes. How can I live with something like this hanging over me?

How can my dad?

"Oh, God," I say, the full effect slamming into me. "I have to tell my dad all of this—my mom."

Finn nods. He's coming back to himself even faster now, and dimly, I realize he's doing it for me. Taking care of me is centering him.

"But Libs? Try not to worry about if this comes out. If it does, we have Carol's statement that she forged the confession's signature, all the documents she collected. We'll fight it and we'll win."

We. One little word and it unlocks my chest. I feel better.

But one glance at Finn and I can tell he's growing tenser by the second. "And all because Carol wanted to be the next Mrs. Oliver." His hands tighten around the steering wheel until it creaks and I rub the back of his neck. Everything is still sinking in, and even though we haven't moved an inch, it feels like the world is sliding.

"I feel sorry for her," I whisper finally.

"I don't. She cheated." He gives me a bitter, *bitter* smile. "Besides, she didn't just screw Maxon. She screwed over my mother, your family."

"And look how she's living now. With all those memories that are turning into nightmares." I shudder. I can't imagine how horrible it must be to fall in love with someone and do terrible things for him and then find out you were only being used."

"You're a better a person than I am." He pauses. "Can you really let that go?"

I want to. I want Carol to have another shot at life and I want my dad to be protected. But the more I want to let the past stay in the past, the more I know I...can't. "No," I say at last. "What happened is horrible and it's dictated the past four years of our lives. My dad is never going to be the same."

Finn's bitter smiles fades and he studies me closely. My stomach squeezes. He's going to let me decide what to do here. I take a deep breath and blow it out slowly. "But the thing is even if we take this to the police, it doesn't get my dad's job back. The embezzling has nothing to do with the contract clause that let Maxon fire him."

"True." But he's still watching me and there's something about the intensity that's almost...frightening. He reaches out, skims his fingers along my cheek. I try to smile and lean into him—which only makes him lighten up. He's touching me like I'm fragile.

Then he leans across the seat and kisses me and there's nothing fragile about it. His hands cup my face, tilting me back for him, open for him. His tongue slides in deep, setting a commanding pace, one that shoots heat straight between my legs. He pushes into me and I welcome him closer, always closer. It's Finn and I can never get enough—and then he pulls back, studying me again.

"Whoa," I whisper. That kiss wasn't just a kiss. That felt like being... Claimed.

I swallow, putting two fingers to my tingling lower lip. "What are you thinking?"

"That I just found leverage on Maxon."

My heart stutters. "What does that mean?"

"He can never keep you from me again."

CHAPTER 26 | Libby

Finn takes me home, but instead of leaving for the city, he stays and helps with barn chores. It should be a really pleasant—albeit chilly—way to spend the afternoon, but he's barely talking to me.

Not that I'm entirely sure what to talk about anyway.

My stomach feels like it's permanently set to churn. I don't know what Finn intends to do with Carol's information and I'm afraid to ask. Even so, I can't stop hearing Finn's words: "He can never keep you from me again."

And every time I do, they ripple up my spine.

"I forget you know how to do this stuff," I say, watching Finn toss down two bales of hay from the loft.

"The horses are important to you." He comes down the ladder, two rungs at a time, and lands at my feet. "You used to say they always came first."

"Yeah," I say softly. Because this means he's putting me first too. My needs always come first for Finn. It's reassuring.

Until I see the tension still simmering in him. He's furious.

"Besides," he adds, "it's nice to be here without...complications."

I nod, but honestly I'm not sure how any of this is going to work. We pulled into the farm as my parents were pulling out. My mom waved, but my dad looked away. I know he'll listen to me about what happened with Carol and the forged confession, but I also know he'll never listen to me about Finn. I saw it in his eyes before he walked out of the kitchen. He doesn't understand how different Maxon and Finn are.

He'll never understand.

I turn my attention to halters hanging up by the double doors, swiping one so I can bring in Drama for dinner.

And also so I don't have to look at Finn. I can't have him without breaking my father's heart and I can't leave him without breaking my own and I'm so lost in the back and forth that I almost miss Finn saying my name.

"Libs?"

"Yeah! Sorry."

"I've been thinking..."

I grin. "You know how I feel about that."

"Funny. I want you to come to the Oliver Holdings party."

"The holiday one?" It's cold in the stable, but I'm suddenly sweating. This is not a good idea. Everyone will see us together. *Maxon* will see us together. "Why do I need to be there? Is this more promo? You giving me some big cardboard check?"

I'm trying for funny and failing. He gives me an inscrutable look. "If you want one. Is that really what you're thinking about right now?"

I bite my lower lip. "No."

"You want to share?"

"Why do you want me to come?"

"Because I want you there."

On any other day, this would make my heart fly sky-high, but after today...it feels like more than just Finn taking us public. It feels like a middle finger to Maxon.

"Why wouldn't you be there? We're together, right? And this is a black-tie thing I have to do every year. I think this year's theme is something to do with carnivals?"

"Gross." I shudder. "Clowns."

He frowns as if this has just now occurred to him. "Very true. Anyway, I want you with me. You'll need a dress." A deeper frown now. He faces me, eyes traveling up my legs to my waist and then to my breasts. Everywhere he looks, I heat.

"Is that wise? I mean, considering what we know now..."

Finn's eyes snap to mine and hold. Suddenly, it isn't the Finn-I-screwed-in-my-truck. It's Finn-the-no-nonsense-businessman. "It's important to me that our employees see where our donations dollars are spent. My father may have flamed our reputation, but I intend to bring it back."

"But—"

"I'll handle it." A shiver rides up my spine. That tone is dangerously close to the one he uses with me when we're messing around and my body goes tight. Finn's gaze rakes up and down me once more. "You don't believe me."

"I didn't say that. I'm just...worried."

Finn nods, walking toward me slowly and deliberately. "I can't have that."

My mouth goes hot. "No."

"You agree?" He licks his lower lip, eyes already focused on my mouth. "Good. I like it when you agree with me."

I grin and shimmy backward. I head for the heated tack room and Finn follows, jerking his shirt loose. It's our game. It's what we do.

And yet something feels different about this time.

Finn's always been demanding and *always* focused on me, but this time...this time there's an intensity I've never felt before. I've barely squirmed out of my jeans and coat before he's slammed the door and is on top of me. He scoops me up, arms under my ass, and puts me down on the desk.

The stable's tack room is usually a sunny place, but Finn yanks the blinds closed, dipping us into dark. The heater's already running, turning the whole space blissfully warm, but my skin stands up in goosebumps when he turns back to me.

"Sweater off," he orders. "Bra on."

I grin, peeling up my sweater to reveal the nearly transparent mesh bra underneath. He swears, palming his hard-on once before walking straight to me.

And pulling down the straps.

And spilling my bare breasts into his hands.

And making me moan.

My knees fall open as I lean back on my hands, heels braced against the desk's edge. He plays with me—twisting and pinching in the way that always makes me wet and desperate. The way that always makes his eyes go bright.

"I love you like this," he murmurs, hands skimming down my sides to explore the edges of my panties—lacy boyshorts today. Understated. Elegant.

Soaked when he skims both thumbs along my core.

I groan and Finn rewards my already aching clit with a dizzying circle. "You need this," he murmurs, his other hand going to his belt.

"I do." Now I'm at his belt too, yanking it loose. "Don't make me wait. Not this time."

"I should make you wait on principle now."

I cup his hard length and his breath leaves him in a long hiss. "You don't want to make me wait either."

A smirk as he rolls on a condom. "I'm always like this for you. I've gotten used to waiting."

"Have you?" I fit both hands around him, pulling him forward until his heated head brushes my soaked panties. "I'm right here," I breathe, rubbing the tip of him up and down me, teasing myself as much as I'm teasing him. "All that stands between us is a scrap of lace."

He groans and pulls back and I think I've lost—he's going to make me wait for it for sure—and then his hands are at my hips. He yanks the boyshorts off me and pulls me to him. I hook my forearm around his neck, delighting in how my sensitive bare breasts rub against his half-unbuttoned dress shirt.

"Ride me hard," I whisper. "Make me scream your name."

Because suddenly I need it. I need him to blot out everything that's happened and everything that might happen. I need the world to be made up only of Finn.

And the pleasure he gives me.

"Always," he whispers and lifts me in his arms—and brings me down on his heated length.

"Yes," I moan, loving how he stretches me and fills me. "Yes! Yes!"

He lifts me up and brings me down again. My clit rubs against him, shooting sparks across my skin. Every thrust is delicious and maddening and driving me relentlessly toward release. I might have gotten my way and Finn's gone straight to satisfying me, but it's his pace, his arms around me, lifting me and lowering me. In his arms, I'm pinned, all I can do is take.

And it's perfect.

"Yesyesyes!" I'm close. I'm *so* close. "Just like that!"

He grips me tighter, pumps me harder. "Open your eyes."

I groan, dragging my heavy lids open to meet his gaze. He's barely holding on. I can see it in his face. I've turned Finn on so many times and in so many ways and this one is about to undo him.

It makes my pussy clench.

Hard.

"You are so fucking perfect," he grates, punctuating each word with a toe-curling thrust. "Watch me as you come, do you understand? Don't look away from me. I want to see it."

I clench again, pleasure rushing up in a wave I cannot stop. "Finn, I'm coming!"

He answers by stroking me harder, firmer. He pushes me over until I'm spiraling, held fast in his arms and spasming against him. Dimly, I'm aware he follows me seconds later. Dimly, I'm aware he's swearing and saying my name and raining kisses across my face and down my neck.

"So good," I mutter, slumping into him. "So good."

His laugh rumbles against my ear. He carefully lowers me back to the desk, holding me steady until I can hold myself. "Kiss me."

Eagerly, I reach up for him. I open my mouth, giving him all of me—and he takes it. Finn kisses me hard and then pushes away. "One second," he murmurs, retreating to the bathroom to clean up. I pull my own clothes back together, smiling like a love-crazed idiot.

Which is pretty much appropriate, I think. I won't be able to hide my feelings if we take this public. Everyone will know as soon as I lay eyes on him.

Maxon will know.

The thought brings me back to my earlier uncertainty. It feels like Finn is rushing this—but not for the right reasons. Is he taking us public because he's truly in love with me?

Or because it's a middle finger to his father?

CHAPTER 27 | Finn

The next day, I pull into the Brays' a little after six in the evening. Winter dark has engulfed the farm and I can barely make out the stable's outline in the shadows. Technically, I could've come sooner, but I wanted to make sure Libby was long gone. She's supposed to be meeting Laurel and Ally tonight and I didn't want to risk running into her—not with what I'm about to do.

I know Libby's anxious about us taking the next step. I could see it in her eyes yesterday. I'd wanted to reassure her, use my body to promise her we'd never be apart again, but then I got a better idea:

We should get married.

After all, it's where we're headed anyway, right? Why not speed things up?

I thought about it all last night and honestly...it's the perfect grand gesture. There is no other way to prove to her—and the rest of the world—how I feel about her. Yeah, I'm not sure about the kind of rings she likes or what kind of wedding she wants, but we can decide all of that later. Right now, I just want her 'yes.'

It's the right move. It's the *only* move.

But I'm still way anxious and it's annoying. I've done multi-billion-dollar deals. I've talked anxious investors off ledges. I've built Oliver Holdings into phenom.

But the prospect of asking Mr. Bray for Libby's hand in marriage is about to make me vomit.

That's probably normal though, right?

Right.

I get out and the cold air hits me like a wall. I flip up my jacket's collar and head for the house. With every step, more and more unease wraps around me and it shouldn't. Marrying Libby is the only sure

point in my life right now. We had four years taken away from us. I'm
not waiting a single minute longer to begin our lives together.

I take the porch steps two at a time and knock on the door. After
a moment, it opens and James's face—even more lined than I remember—appears in the crack of space.

"You have a lot of nerve," he says, looking about two seconds away
from slamming the door on me. "What do you want?"

"A moment of your time." I pause, feeling my insides winding
tighter and tighter. "Can I come in?"

"Whatever you have to say to me, you can say it from there."

"Please, James. We used to be more than this." Not my most impressive show of charm, but he seems to think it over, and finally, he nods
and takes a few steps back, taking a sip of his Scotch and opening the
door just enough for me to slide through. There's faint music coming
from the kitchen down the hallway—Mrs. Bray no doubt, maybe working on a recipe, maybe preparing dinner.

Please don't hear us, I pray and turn to James.

"Sir," I say. I don't bother taking off my coat and he doesn't bother
asking me to. I just get right to it. "I'm sorry about the way things have
fallen out between us, but I hope we can move forward from it."

"You're kidding me."

"No, I'm not. I want to apologize and move forward."

"And why would we do that?" There's a flicker of recognition in his
eyes and my stomach churns uneasily. He knows why.

Which means we both know what's coming.

That should be a good thing, but it doesn't feel like it. As I open my
mouth to speak, James's hand tightens around his drink. He looks half
a second away from punching me.

I go for it anyway: "I'd like us to move forward because I love your
daughter more than anything and I want to marry her and...I want to
ask your permission before I ask her." I barely sound like me, but maybe
that's a good thing. My voice has gone so even, so distant, I could be

delivering a PowerPoint presentation or closing a deal. I could be anyone—and that has to be for the best because I know he looks at me and sees Maxon.

"She values your opinion very much," I add, hating it and knowing it's true at the same time. "I know she won't consider me without your blessing. Family means everything to Libby."

James works his jaw from side to side, different responses zinging through his eyes like ticker-tape. "No," he says at last, rattling the ice in his Scotch glass. In the kitchen, Mrs. Bray changes the music from classical to Dean Martin. Briefly, he glances in her direction, but she doesn't appear at the door. She hasn't heard us.

"I can't do that," he adds.

"Why not?"

"I don't owe you an explanation."

I stiffen. "Yeah, you do. Thanks to me, your daughter knows the truth about what happened. She doesn't think you're an embezzler who involved her in his crimes."

"And thanks to you, she knows about it *period*."

It's true, and for a moment, there's nothing between us but glaring and hard breathing. I have the irrational urge to punch him and I'd be willing to bet money he feels the same.

"And," he says at last. "Your father is a philandering sociopath. He'll go through anyone to get what he wants and I don't believe for a moment you don't have the same tendencies."

For a second, the world jerks out from under my feet. I realize my fists have clenched and I have to force my hands to shake loose. "Tendencies? You have an example for that?"

He thinks it over and finally shrugs. "No. I don't. Yet. You were good to my daughter for a time, but you also took off. Not to mention, you share half your genes with Maxon Oliver and I'm willing to lay odds that eventually you'll be just like him. You can't help it."

All my air has left me. It's worse than being punched. My worst nightmare is becoming Maxon Oliver and the idea that someone else thinks it's my destiny? It's sickening.

Worse than sickening because this isn't just about me. It's about Libby. I know she'll never agree to marry me without his consent. After the false confession, I know she feels guilty and obligated.

And I'm going to lose her, I think, mouth going dry.

James smiles like he knows I'm putting it all together. "Do you have anything else you'd like to say to me?"

"No, I think we both know where we stand now."

"Good. Now get out."

My instincts are to call Libby and tell her we're done. I mean, we have to be, right? Her parents mean the world to her, and if they can't forgive me, there's no future for us? It feels like cold truth. My brain is telling me this is logical.

But she once told me my brain lies—and this has to be one of those times. I gave Libby up once because I thought it was the noble thing to do. This time? This time, I'll tell her everything and we'll work it out together.

Because there was always an us. Even when there wasn't.

CHAPTER 28 | Libby

"That's it!" I call to the tiny blonde riding by on Drama. The little girl finally has some momentum going and she's finding her rhythm. "Good job!"

Bridget nods, mouth set into a determined line. Kid kills me in the best way. I always look forward to their morning lessons—even if I'm tired from being out with the girls from the night before.

"Push your heels down and keep your eyes up!" I remind her as she passes me. Bridget nods again, but then her brother—riding the long-suffering Al Capony—swerves into their path. I'd like to say it was an accident, but Brody's been in a mood ever since he arrived for his lesson and I suspect he's trying to get a rise out of his twin sister.

Not a hugely difficult thing to do, honestly. Both children have pretty serious tempers—and I would never admit it, but I kind of sort of find their swearing adorable because they do it in tiny Irish accents. They only arrived in the States a year or so ago.

"If he's not careful, she's going to deck him," a voice mutters. I glance behind me, spotting Parker standing by the arena fence. Most people would be a bit horrified to be responsible for wrangling the Macken twins, but Parker always looks a bit amused. "Of course, then," she continues, "he'll hit her back and we'll have a brawl on our hands."

The idea makes all the color drain from my face, but Parker—who started out as the twins' nanny but will probably end up being their aunt—grins. Curvy with dark hair and darker eyes, she's always reminds me of a vintage pin-up girl even though she favors skinny jeans and Frye boots and soft, slouchy sweaters. It's a gorgeous look on her and I always catch myself making a note of what she's wearing. It seems so effortless—doesn't hurt that she's always glowing.

Then again, she's seriously dating one of the most gorgeous riders on the circuit: Irish showjumper, Aiden Macken. I'd probably be glowing all the time too.

There's a crunch of gravel and I turn to see Finn driving in. My grin is immediate. I can actually feel myself to lighter. Brighter.

He wasn't supposed to come by today. What an awesome surprise.

I turn my attention back to the kids and tell my fluttering stomach to stand down. I need to concentrate. "Okay, you two," I call, taking a few steps toward the kids. "Turn left, halt in the center of the arena, and pat your ponies. They were rock stars today."

"So was I," Brody says, expertly turning Al toward me and slowing him to a halt.

"You were, huh?" I ask, trying not to smile.

Parker rolls her eyes. "The Macken men, I swear. Brody? It's called being humble. We're going to talk about it in the car."

"Thanks a lot, stupid," Bridget says, halting Drama next to him. "Now we're going to get a lecture."

"Don't call your brother 'stupid,'" Parker says, running a hand through her short-cropped hair. Anyone else would be sounding frazzled at this point, but she seems rather amused by the whole thing.

Brody glares at his sister like he wants to set her on fire. Bridget smirks.

"Tough crowd," Finn says and the words tip-toe up my spine. Ugh. That voice of his is practically indecent. It's so deep and gravely and...freaking sexy. I can feel my nipples already hardening.

"Hey," I say, holding Drama with one hand while helping Bridget dismount. She slides to the ground and takes her pony's reins and I turn to hold Al for Brody. The ponies are safe as houses, but the twins have only been riding for a few months now and I still take the extra precaution. "I didn't expect you to stop by," I add.

Finn smiles, but the smile doesn't reach his eyes and worry prickles me. Is something wrong? I help Brody lift Al's reins over his head so he can lead the pony to the gate and Bridget follows us.

"Miss Libby," she says, "Can we put glitter on Drama's hooves next time? She would look smashing in hot pink."

"You think everyone looks smashing in hot pink," Brody counters.

"Because it's true!"

"*Isn't!*"

"*Is!*"

Parker groans. "Stand down, you two." She turns to Finn and offers him a gloved hand. "Parker Waye. Pretty sure we're Libby's most obnoxious clients."

I burst out laughing. "Not by a long shot."

She grins and Finn takes her hand. "Finn Oliver," he says. "Nice to meet you."

They spend the next twenty minutes or so chatting while the twins and I get the ponies put away. It isn't too hard. The twins are so young and so new to riding, we haven't done much to make Al and Drama break a sweat. We spend most of the time fluffing up their winter coats with stiff brushes and giving them their evening grain.

"Al is the best pony ever," Brody announces.

"No, he's not," Bridget says, shoving her twin hard enough to make him stagger.

"Yes, he is!" Brody spins around to shove her back and I pick him up, his little arms pinwheeling as he tries to swipe at his sister.

"Knock it off," I tell him. "Or I'll carry you around like a baby until Parker's ready to leave."

Brody arches a brow, looking for all the world like a little old man. "Bet you'll get tired of that before I do."

I stuff down a laugh. Between Brody's Irish accent and general attitude, the kid can always make me smile, but in this case, he's absolutely right. I'd thought being carried would embarrass him, but Brody is pretty much immune to embarrassment.

I lean in so our noses almost brush. "True, but I can make you clean stalls until your fingers freeze."

He pauses, thinking this over. "Ach. Fine. You've made your point."

I put him down and he runs off, Bridget hot behind him, heading for Parker's shiny-new Jeep. "Oh boy, I better go," she says, eyes gone huge. "I'll see you next week," she calls to me, dashing after them.

"Bye!" I wave, and for a minute, Finn and I watch the three of them pile into the car before driving off. The last thing I see before Parker turns out of sight is the outline of Bridget sucker-punching her brother.

He's going to get her back for that one, I think.

Finn turns to me, hands in his overcoat's pockets. "She seems nice."

"She is."

"I like the lights," he says, glancing up at the strands of multi-colored Christmas lights I've strung along the tops of the stalls and criss-crossed above the aisle. They cast reds and greens and yellows across his gorgeous face. "Festive."

I grin. "I thought so. Maybe we should add mistletoe."

"Maybe you should."

He should be smiling, I think, stomach sinking and sinking. Why isn't he smiling? Finn looks at me. I look at him. Something's wrong. I don't know what, but something's off. I stretch my grin a little wider even as my stomach plunges an inch. "You okay?"

"Had better days."

I hesitate. "Do you want to talk about it?"

"No." His eyes are boring holes into me and I have the strangest feeling he's memorizing me, like he feels I'm about to disappear. "I don't want to talk about it. I want to marry you."

CHAPTER 29 | Libby

"I don't want to talk about it," he says. "I want to marry you."

My heart rides up my throat, choking me. "What?" I manage, sounding little and faraway. I didn't expect this. I hadn't even thought about it.

Finn watches me, something sad creeping into his eyes. I have the most horrible feeling he expected this. "Marry me, Libs. Will you marry me? Please say yes."

His gaze is still pinned to me and I want to say yes. I want to say yes a million times and yet...why does this feel off?

Very, *very* off.

I try to swallow, but my mouth has gone cotton dry. I put one hand on the stall next to me, steadying myself. "Finn, of course I want to say yes, but..."

"Libs, now is not the time for buts."

"But did you ask my dad?" He flinches like I've slapped him and I rush to explain. "It's just that whenever I imagined my wedding, it was always with my parents' blessing. You asked...right?"

He studies me, saying nothing, and I suddenly have my answer. He did ask. My dad said no.

"I—I—I don't know what to say," I manage at last.

Another flinch. Definitely not what Finn wanted to hear. My whole body goes cold in a way that has nothing to do with winter. I'm losing feeling in my hands...my feet...my face. This is awful and I never saw it coming.

"Finn." I take a step toward him and he takes a step back. "I didn't mean it like that," I explain, pulse pounding. "I don't know where to have myself right now. I'm...stunned."

It's true too. This should be an amazing moment. I should be over the moon with happiness—the man I love beyond measure just asked me to marry him—but I'm also torn. My family doesn't want me to marry him? My dad really said no? How awful. Yes or no, I will hurt someone I love.

It wasn't supposed to be like this.

"He really said no?" I ask at last, clenching my hands at my side.

"He did."

My stomach swoops into my feet. I'm not sure which is scarier to me: looking at Finn's expressionless face or imagining my father's enraged reaction. We're barely speaking. I can't imagine a worse time to ask him.

But that's another matter. Right now, I need to fix things with Finn. But how? I don't know what to do or what to say, but I know I need something—something true and genuine and *right*—otherwise I'm going to lose Finn.

Or maybe I already have.

Because there's no coming back from this, is there? I realize. I turn him down and he'll ghost for good.

"I knew it meant a lot to you," Finn says, hands going to his pockets even though I *wish* he'd reach for me. "I wanted to honor that."

"Let me talk to him," I say at last, focusing on the tasseled ends of my scarf so I don't have to meet Finn's eyes. "I don't want things to be like this. He'll come around—"

"He's not coming around, Libs. You want me, you're going to have to accept that."

I freeze and slowly—slowly—I look up at him. "I do want you."

"Is that my yes?"

Tears prick my eyes. "No."

His whole body stills. The wind picks up, rushing down the stable aisle and swirling around us and I barely feel it.

I barely feel anything. My whole body's gone numb.

"You can't have it both ways," he says at last. "You can't have me and them."

"I'm not trying to. I'm asking...for time. That's all. Just a little bit of time to talk to him. He will come around. I know he will. I just need a little more time for him to see—"

"Take all the time you need," Finn says, voice distant as he straightens. One hand returns to his pocket, pulling out his car keys.

Leaving, I realize. He's leaving because he doesn't believe you.

I stumble forward, reaching for him. "Finn—"

"Don't." He shies away from my hand. "You can't..." He blows out a sigh, still refusing to look at me. "Please don't touch me. If you do, it makes it harder to do the right thing."

"What?"

His eyes meet mine. "I don't want to be the final thing that destroys your family, Libs."

"You aren't."

"I am. I will be. You have to choose us because you want us—and you're going to have to want it with all your heart." He pauses, eyes glittering with need. "Want me."

It kicks the air from my lungs. "Wanting you has never been the problem."

And maybe it's the word 'problem' or maybe it's my brain finally catching up, but I suddenly don't understand why he asked me to marry him. Why now? What changed?

Because he knows the kind of man Maxon Oliver really is, I think. Because he's going to rub you in his father's face.

This isn't love—not entirely. I know without a doubt Finn loves me, but he's also in love with the idea of revenge. Even if he doesn't know it yet.

"Why are you asking to get married now?" My voice is surprisingly level for someone who feels like she's spinning. "We just got back together."

"We both know where this was going—or I thought we did."

I'm not the only one going level. Finn suddenly sounds like he's in a business meeting, like he's analyzing the pros and cons of a buy-out, and my spine stiffens. I don't want yelling or crying, but I don't want to be a logical next move either. It only makes me think this really is a way to stick-it to Maxon. It's the perfect follow-up.

"I still don't understand," I say, easing toward him even as he eases away from me. Now, we're circling each other. "You know where my dad is right now. You know he's upset and you chose now to ask him?"

"I wanted the gesture."

I blink. Ah. Finn and his grand gestures. Gorgeous hotel rooms and rented out theaters and kisses that make me feel like I'm more than myself.

"This is about more than a gesture," I whisper. "You need to get your head straight. Please, Finn, I don't think you're doing this for the right reason."

And as soon as I say it, I know I believe it with all my heart.

"Can you really look at me and tell me this has nothing to do with Maxon?"

"Fuck Maxon."

It's like a blow. For a second, I feel sick. There's your answer, I think. "No. No way. You're still angry and I want you to be with me because of *me*. Not because you want to spite your dad."

He stops, watching me like a hunter would watch a fawn. I don't like it. He's pulling away and I can feel myself slipping. "You need time to think," I whisper. "Please? Take some time?"

He doesn't answer. In fact, he doesn't say a single word. Finn walks out and it drags pieces of me with him.

CHAPTER 30 | Finn

Get my head straight. Right. And how do I do that when the one person who does straighten out my head won't talk to me? I spend the first hour after my fight with Libby being furious with her.

And then I get it.

I *do* need to get my head straight and it isn't cool that I lean so hard on her to do it. But the thing is, I don't actually know how to fix myself.

I know how to work. I know how to love Libby. I know how to do those two things so well they blot out everything else. But fix me? No clue.

"You need to take better care of yourself." It's my mom's voice in my head, but it's so clear she might as well have been sitting right in the car next to me. She used to say that to me all the time—especially when I was working too hard. When I was little, she'd take me out for walks on the property. We'd linger in the woods or sit by one of the streams that ran through our fields, watching tadpoles. It had to be boring as hell for her—sometimes we were out for hours before I could calm down—but she always did it.

And just like that I know where I need to go.

To her.

***

We buried my mom in a historic cemetery not far from the house. There might have been grander places, but I don't think we could've found anywhere more beautiful. Even in early winter, the sunny hilltop is alive with birds and there are deer grazing by the forest's edge. She would've loved that. She really enjoyed animals—would come to Libby's horse shows even though horses terrified her.

It's a damn shame I haven't been by more.

Or at all.

I stare down at her headstone and study the fresh flowers someone's left. They're roses of some type, white and over-perfumed. I don't know that she would've picked them out herself, but they're here and they're beautiful.

And they're more than you brought, I remind myself, sinking to my knees. Cold ground bites through my pants, but I stay put. I should've come before now. I should've come so many times before now.

"Mom," I say, testing out the idea. It feels incredibly stupid to be talking to myself, but maybe it's all the quiet or maybe I'm cracking up because I almost don't feel like I'm talking to myself. It almost feels like she's here. "I don't know what to do."

A cloud passes over the sun, coating me in pale shadows. I take a couple deep breaths and try to decide where to begin because 'I don't know what to do' isn't really the truth, is it?

"I know what I *want* to do," I continue, keeping my eyes on the wooded horizon. "I want to make him pay. This forged confession thing...it's a whole new low—and we already knew he was a piece of shit, didn't we?" I catch myself looking around for her, looking for her wry smile of agreement. I can't imagine what it's like to be married to someone who cheats.

I don't want to imagine it. Watching her live through it was bad enough.

"It isn't just about getting revenge for the Brays," I add, somehow this is becoming easier, the words coming faster. "It's about everyone else he's hurt—you, me, there must be more victims. How many other people has he hurt?"

The sheer uncertainty of it threatens to make my stomach upend. I shake myself and try to re-center. "Point is, he gets away with it! Again and again. That has to stop. *I* have to stop him."

And the realization stops me. I spend a few minutes running my hand over the grass. A cold breeze snakes across the field and nudges under all my clothes. "That's crazy though, isn't it? I could confront him with the truth until the fucking cows come home and he isn't going to change. The only thing I can do is change myself—which I have. I've already shown Libby that I'm not the same guy."

Only as soon as I say I wonder if I have. I've spent a lot of time doing the things that would impress Merrick's women. I haven't been able to do the things I know would impress Libby. Farm chores the other day was the closest thing to it and I was so preoccupied with thinking about my dad and worrying about Libby's reaction that I snapped. I jumped her instead of telling her how I felt. I used my body to tell her how I felt. I didn't use my mouth.

Well, I *did* use my mouth, but not the way I should have, I think, frowning. I'm starting to see where Libby was coming from today when she told me this felt sudden, like it was more about Maxon and less about her.

I haven't told her how I feel. I've taken care of her. I've given her things. Hell, I've worshiped her body until I damn near had nothing left, but I've never told her what she means to me.

"I can fix that," I say, taking a deep breath and then another. Until now, I didn't realize how tight my chest was, how shallow my breath had become. Not surprising I guess that thinking about Libby would make everything slow down. "I'll tell her how I really feel and the proposal isn't a grand gesture to piss off Maxon, it's doing something I would've done years ago if we hadn't split and—"

And I'm going to have to settle things with Maxon before she believes that. The realization hits me dead-on and my whole body tenses. The cold is seeping through my clothes now, but I can barely feel it.

"I don't know how to settle things," I manage at last. "I want to hurt him. He deserves it. All those promises he's made to employees, to you, to fucking *Carol*." I pause. Libby must really be rubbing off on me if I can feel an iota of sympathy for Carol. "He made promises to her and she believed him and yeah, her character sucks, but I still feel a bit sad for her. I know you would too."

It's the truth, too.

All those women my father screwed, my mother actually felt a bit sad for them. They were looking for something and they weren't going to find it with Maxon. She was gracious like that, could see the agony in another person when all I could see was the deceit.

I sit up straight, another realization hitting me full-on. "No fucking wonder you love Libby—sorry. I know you hate it when I swear."

And then I catch myself: loved, not love. Hated it, not hate it. Briefly, it's like losing her all over again and the pain of it chokes me.

"All those women he screwed behind your back. All those times he hurt you..." I trail off, a lifetime of memories rushing back.

Maxon making her cry.

Maxon making promises.

Maxon breaking every single one.

The clouds slide away from the sun and I watch the shadows rush away. This is our family legacy, I think. Only...maybe it *was* our family legacy. Maybe Libby and I can change that.

"I don't suppose you have any suggestions aside from groveling?" I ask, tilting my face toward the sunshine. I close my eyes and the backs of my lids go dark pink. "Going to take that as a no," I decide and push to my feet, shaking off the cold.

I feel better—chilled—but better. I should come see her more often—and the guilt of not coming before now rushes to my surface again. Honestly? I couldn't bring myself to come. It seemed horrible, an ugly reminder of what I'd lost.

Now though...now I feel like I still have something here.

"I love you, Mom. I always will." I turn toward my car, barely down the hill before I see a dark blue SUV crest the road. It pulls up to the cemetery fence and my stomach clenches.

Why are they here? What's going on? I keep moving even though anger's starting to boil in me and when I'm ten strides—eight strides?—away, they climb out.

Mrs. Bray reaches me first. "Finn, can we talk?"

CHAPTER 31 | Finn

We can talk, but what's there to say? Briefly, I consider telling Mrs. Bray to leave it. This is done. You can break things you will never get back and this thing between us? It's one of them and we *both* had a hand in destroying it. But there's something about her expression that stops me dead.

She looks absolutely agonized and her hand's ice-cold when she touches my arm. "Finn, can we talk?"

I pause, already turning my car keys around and around in my hand. This feels like an ambush. I can't tell what's coming, but I'm pretty sure whatever it is, I'm not going to like it. "Of course."

"James told me about...what you asked...how you wanted—*want* to marry Libby."

I don't say anything. Some of this is because I don't know what to say. The rest of my silence is because of James Bray. He's just come around the SUV's front and is staring me down. There's something uncertain in his eyes.

"And?" I ask Mrs. Bray.

"And I can't tell you how happy that makes me!" Tears streak down her cheeks and she beams at me. "It's everything I've wanted for her."

I blink. I have no idea what to say to that. Of all the things I expected to hear...

She steps a little closer, mouth tight with emotion. "It's everything we've both wanted for her."

Ah. Since when? I want to ask. I cut my eyes to James. He nods. "I owe you an apology, Finn. I blew up really hard and took it out on you."

"It's fine. I can understand why."

"No, no." He shakes his head, walking around his SUV to loop one arm around his wife's shoulders. "It's not fine. I took the whole thing so personally—we have history, you know?"

I do, but I stay quiet because James seems like he needs to get this out. He's holding onto Elizabeth like she's a lifeline and looking at me like I have all the answers. "You were like a son to me. I was so invested in you. I could see your greatness early on—it was my idea to sign you up for Little League."

I smile. I can't help it. *That* had been a disaster. Teamwork has never been my thing and Little League baseball is pretty much entirely teamwork. James had dropped me off and picked me up for all the preseason practices and was thrilled when he got to watch my game—and then horribly disappointed when he realized all the coach did was yell incoherently.

"Did you learn anything about teamwork?" he'd asked as we walked back to the parking lot.

"Yeah," I'd said. "If you have a team, there's always someone else to blame."

James had pulled me that same day. We did other stuff after that—batting cages, golf, a few rounds with paintball guns—but after my mom had gotten sick, I'd stuck close to her, taking care of things.

And of course watching out for Maxon.

"When you asked to become part of our family," James continues, "I should have said you were already family. You always have been—"

"And you're like family to me," I say. "What Maxon threatened, what he was going to do to you...I couldn't let it happen."

James flinches and I can see the truth of it in his eyes.

"I know," Elizabeth says. "*We* know. You did a noble thing, honey. You sacrificed yourself to save us."

"Rather pointless gesture though, wasn't it?" I lean back against my car, crossing my arms and fighting down a surge of disgust. "I'm angry with myself for not seeing through Maxon. I don't know why I didn't question him more. I don't know why I believed him."

"I'm glad you did."

James and I turn to Elizabeth. She nods. "I'm glad you did. If you had pushed him, he would've cut you off. You would have lost your father and your mother. As terrible as this is, it would've been worse if you had done it earlier."

For a second, I don't know what to say. She's right. Holy shit is she ever right. My mom was going through her last round of treatments. It wasn't too long after I broke things off with Libby that she took a turn for the worse.

And not long after that...we lost her.

"He played on your love for Libby," Elizabeth continues, eyes shining with unshed tears. "That says everything about him and everything about you."

"That I'm easily manipulated?" I mean it as a joke, but Elizabeth isn't in the mood. Her whole expression turns thunderous.

"Finn Oliver, you're an honest person. You treat others honestly, and as a result, you expect others to behave the same way. I would rather have you like this than anything like Maxon."

We study each other. I'm a good enough poker player and businessman that I know my expression is giving her jack shit to go on right now and I'm glad. Her words have punched holes straight through me.

And hit bone.

"I...appreciate that." Which is beyond true and beyond inadequate for what she just let loose inside me. I feel like I'm walking around myself, suddenly seeing me as she sees me.

James nods. "I agree with Elizabeth, Finn. When I stepped back and looked at the situation, I couldn't be more proud and more heartbroken for you."

We all go quiet, and in the silence, Elizabeth edges a little closer. "Have you told Libby what happened between you and James?"

"Yeah."

They both wince and I rush to reassure them: "Don't. It's not your fault. She said no, but it isn't entirely because of James and me, she...doubts my sincerity."

"Your sincerity?" Elizabeth echoes, mouth rounding. "Of all the things Libby would doubt that...surprises me. A lot."

"She wanted me to think it over," I add.

"Have you?"

"Yeah, but I'm not sure I can reassure her."

"Try again," James says, clapping one hand to my upper arm and for a moment, this is four years ago, five, longer and I feel my whole world tilt back into focus. I hadn't realized how much I'd missed them until now. "You have more than our blessing to marry our daughter. You have our all our hopes for you."

"Ask her again, Finn," Elizabeth whispers. "Ask her again."

I smile, but don't answer. There's another side to this—Maxon—and that will stop Libby from saying yes just as much as her parents' disapproval. Our relationship hinges on certain requirements. The thing between us has always been a back-and-forth, something that can drown me and sustain me.

The thing between Maxon and me is similar, isn't it? I've survived this long with him. I hate him, but I don't cut him loose because of the fallout.

I say my good-byes to the Brays and I let them pull out first, watching their taillights disappear before turning the Audi's ignition. The engine comes alive, heater starting up full-blast. I warm my fingers against the hot air and check my phone, hoping to see a missed call from Libby. Nothing though—there is one text. It's from Merrick:

Call me ASAP. Your dad knows

I study the screen for a minute...a minute more...and then it hits me. *Everything* hits me. I text back:

Good because I'm on my way to finish this

CHAPTER 32 | Libby

"Wait." Laurel holds her martini inches from her mouth and blinks at me. It's been hours and hours after Finn walked out on me. I'm cleaned up, scrubbed up, and out to dinner with my best friends. I should feel amazing.

And I don't. Honestly, I feel pretty close to crying, but the tears won't come and I can't decide if I'm grateful or disappointed.

Laurel puts her martini down and places both hands on the table-top. Her silver thumb-ring winks under the overhead lights. "Finn Oliver asked you to marry him and you said you needed *time?*"

"Technically, I told him he needed to get his head on straight," I clarify.

The girls look at me. I look back, replaying in my head how that sounds and...yeah. There's no way to spin this that will look good.

"I'm going to need another drink," Ally announces, lifting one hand to attract our waitress's attention. Tonight, she's wearing an open-back white sweater that shows off her toned shoulders and tanned skin to perfection and I catch myself wondering if Finn would like me to wear something like that.

And then I remind myself that it might not matter.

Not anymore.

"Wait," Ally says, eyeing me. "Maybe *you* need the second drink more than I do."

"Ha ha. I know what I said to him sounds crazy. I feel kind of crazy. Everything's happened really fast." I take a deep breath and focus on my roasted chicken for a minute. We're at Pascal's in Peachtree City, a small suburb south of Atlanta. The place is tiny and quiet and while that's all kinds of perfect for meeting the girls for dinner, it's pretty much a terrible place for a meltdown. Other customers will definitely notice and someone will post a Yelp review about how their dinner was great, but they could do without the crying girl in the corner.

"But the timing of his proposal seems so convenient," I add. "Plus, my parents are against it and there's...everything else."

Laurel doesn't look like she agrees at all, but true to form, she doesn't say anything more and pretends to be extremely interested in the beaded edge on her sleeve. Honestly, I get where she's coming from. I've been in love with Finn for...well, forever so this should've been the happiest development ever and I ruined it.

Or my dad ruined it.

Or everything around us ruined it.

I can't really decide actually.

So I stuff another piece of crusty bread into my mouth and Ally watches me chew. She has a look on her face that I know too well. It's either 'I am about to drop some wisdom on you' or 'I told you so' and I'm not in the mood for either.

"I know y'all think he's horrible," I say. "And I get that. I do. But I really think we have something special. It's just the timing of everything and—"

"You convincing us or you?" Ally asks and takes a big sip of her lemon drop. Our waitress stops by and everyone orders another round.

"You're annoying," I tell Ally as soon as she leaves with our drink orders. It's true too, but I can't stop my smile.

She grins too. "Libs, I gotta say...you've been in love with this guy since we met and now you're together again and something's in the way because of *course* something's in the way and now you have to make a decision."

Nausea sweeps through me and I concentrate on dabbing away the sweat from my chilled peach martini. Why can't our love go the way it's supposed to go? Why does everything have to be so hard? And, worst of all, why do I have to choose between two people who mean so much to me?

"So it all comes down to a decision?" I ask, taking another ferocious bite of bread. Usually, it's delicious, but right now it's like cardboard in my mouth. "My father or Finn?"

She shrugs, expression turning sad. "It looks like it—at least for the moment. Honestly, I think your dad will come around, but if you turn down Finn, it's done. There's no coming back from this."

Laurel nods. She drags her spoon through her soup in smaller and smaller circles. "This is really awful. I'm so sorry, Libs."

"Me too," Ally adds.

For a beat, we sit in silence and then I force myself to straighten. "In the meantime, I have to find a dress for the Oliver Holdings' holiday party. Either of you up for shopping? I was thinking about hitting some of the consignment shops."

"I'm always up for shopping," Ally says, twirling the end of one braid around her. "But why don't you try on some of my stuff first. I have a cobalt blue dress that would look amazing on you."

"I'd really appreciate it."

"'Course." She glances at Laurel and Laurel raises one auburn brow. She might never offer unsolicited advice, but no one is above a sketchy look.

"What?" I ask.

Another glance between them.

"*What?*"

"Why are you going to the party now?" Laurel asks, picking at her napkin and clearly uncomfortable with asking me about. "This whole thing was supposed to be secret and you were both good with that. What changed?"

Unease flickers in me. "We can be in the open now, I guess. Before, he was worried about attracting his dad's attention. Now, it doesn't matter."

"You're going to have to fill me in on that one," Laurel says and I do, going from the huge blow-up with my parents to confronting Carol to Finn saying he now had leverage on his father.

"What if proposing to me is some sort of...revenge?"

"Is he the type to do that?"

"I don't know. He's really angry though. Really. Angry."

"I don't know." Ally swirls her Lemon Drop around and around until it's a yellow tornado inside the martini glass. "Finn's a lot of things, but he isn't stupid and it would be incredibly stupid to propose marriage just to get back at someone."

"Yeah."

"Is that all that's bothering you? Seems like there's more to it."

"I guess, I'm just worried that now everyone will see we're together and everyone will know we're together and..." Just say it, I tell myself, feeling heat climb my cheeks. "And it's going to be even more painful and humiliating when we break up."

"When you break up? Since when is that a given?"

I blink. Actually, I don't know. Since...always?

"Honey," Ally says, shaking her head, "if you have one foot out the door, this is never going to work. Finn seems like he's all in. Yeah, the proposal might've been a little fast and maybe Maxon has a part in it, but he's been pretty much perfect otherwise."

I play with the edge of my napkin until I can trust myself to speak again. "So what do I do?"

"Trust your heart."

"But I don't know what my heart wants!"

Ally quirks one brow. "You sure about that?"

"Yeah," I say, but I know I'm lying. I know exactly what my heart wants.

I'm just not sure how to make it happen.

CHAPTER 33 | Finn

Architectural Digest once called our house 'a vision of warm lights and airy spaces,' but right now it's dark and the four stories seem impossibly close to the ground. I swing my car through the wrought-iron gates and gas it up the drive.

"Are you sure this is a good idea?" Merrick asks, his voice sounding a bit tinny coming through the Bluetooth speaker system. "You sound like you're driving like a maniac."

"That's because you drive like an old lady."

"I'm trying not to get pulled over. I drive a red Porsche. It's like cat-nip for police officers."

"Nothing about that car says 'cat-nip.' Inadequate penis size on the other hand? Yes."

"Bitchy. Nice. You're clearly in a great state of mind to confront your father."

I scowl. I hate it when he's right. I downshift for the last turn. "Maybe it'll work in my favor this time."

"Yeah, maybe," Merrick returns in a tone that pretty much says 'no way.' "Good luck."

For once, I don't need it, I think, disconnecting. Forget luck. I have the truth. It's way better.

I take the looping driveway around to main house's garage and park where my mom used to leave her car.

The reminder spikes sour points in the back of my mouth and I stride across the courtyard, pocketing a copy of the fake confession, and let myself into the house. The kitchen's dark. The sitting room's dark. The sunroom, the study, the open-air foyer, all dark.

Then I realize Maxon has taken this back to where it all began: his office, when he ranted about James embezzling money and extracted promises from me.

Good, I think, pivoting toward the house's eastern wing. I like symmetry.

I also like how he thinks he has the upper hand when he doesn't. I hadn't planned on confronting him so quickly, but Merrick's text let me know I needed to move fast.

"Can't I come with you?" Libby had asked as I'd quickly dressed. "You came with me when I told my parents."

"Maxon isn't the same thing as your parents."

She'd gone quiet, had probably been considering all the ways our family situations had never been the same when she'd suddenly said: "I'm scared."

It had pulled me into pieces. I never want her to be scared. I never want her to worry. I'd pulled her into my arms and held her until I had to put her away because I was worried I'd never leave otherwise.

"He can't hurt us anymore, Libs."

She'd hesitated. "But you can, if you make this about revenge."

"It's not about revenge."

And it wasn't—isn't. But I'd be lying if I said shoving the fake confession in his face wouldn't be deeply satisfying. So much so it actually quickens my pace down the winding hallway that leads to his office. I wrench open the heavy double doors and Maxon's sitting at his desk, glaring at me like I'm an employee he's about to fire.

He leans forward and spits, "I found that contract for your new little pet project. I told you you were done with that girl."

Drunk, I realize, looking him over. How James can think we're anything alike baffles me. The man before me is blotchy with drink and has hate in his eyes. Even at my worst, I never looked like this.

It's almost reassuring until he pitches a pen in my direction. "Are you listening to me?" he yells. "I said you were done with her."

"You did." I don't bother closing the door behind me—the house is deserted now except for him—and drop into the chair across from him, ready to play this out. I don't have to placate him, not anymore. "But that was before you decided to tank our company—and nearly all our employees—with a racist rant."

"Who cares about the employees? If they don't like it here, they can move on."

"I care, Dad. I. Care. Most of their retirement plans are tied up in Oliver Holdings' stock. You know that. Your tantrum didn't just screw our family's bank account. It screwed all of theirs as well."

"Such a bleeding heart."

I start to respond and then decide against it. He's drunk. There's no point. Yeah, he's right. There are plenty of worthy causes we could support. I went back to Libby because it was Libby. It's always been Libby for me.

And it'll always be Libby for me in the future.

The thought makes me smile.

He can't take her from me. Not anymore. I don't have to put up with his manipulations or lies any longer.

Even better...he'll owe me. Now I have leverage—and I can feel my smile stretch into a grin.

"Are you high?" he demands. "Whatever you're thinking, say it."

"Excellent. Because I want to talk about James Bray." I flick the confession onto his desk and wait for him to recognize it. Thanks to all the Scotch and god-knows-what-else, it takes a minute, but when he does, his mouth flattens.

"What about it?" he asks at last.

"You had Carol Wright forge his signature to a false confession."

"And?"

"And you told me that was the reason you fired him. He was embezzling and you were going to turn him in."

Nothing. No response. He's watching me, waiting to see what I'm going to do with this and satisfaction rolls hot and hard through my chest. Good. I'm glad he's willing to wait. Because this is how things are going to go:

"Maxon," I begin, settling into the chair. The office smells faintly of his cigars and leather cleaner. Usually, it sets my teeth on edge. Now, I feel like I could stay all day. "You just forfeited any right to dictate terms with me. I have you dead to rights—"

"Who says? You can't prove anything!"

"I have a witness who can." I pause, waiting for that to hit him and then drop the next, "Plus, all of her research." I made a tsk-ing noise as I watch recognition finally hit him. It makes his eyes go wide. "That's right. Carol. I tracked it back to her, and turns out, she's really regretting how things were left."

"She's crazy. She'll say anything. Why do you think I let her go?"

"Interesting how many crazy people you've employed over the years. You seem to have quite the habit—or is it that you're the dishonest one and this is the only way you can discredit them?" I pause, waiting for his response and there isn't one. He's watching me, waiting. "You were embezzling the money, weren't you?"

Again, nothing. But sometimes nothing says everything and satisfaction hits me square on. "You blamed him to cover yourself. Nice. Really says a lot about you. Listen, this is how things are going to go from now on...you're done with me. You have no hold, no say-so, no opinion. You break any of that? I take everything public. Everything. Do you understand?"

His nostrils flare. "You think this is over?" he asks, eyes glittering in the low light. "It isn't over. It's just beginning."

I shake my head. There's no point in arguing—not because he's right, but because it's truly done.

And for the first time in my life, I walk away. Free.

CHAPTER 34 | Libby

The twins are more focused in today's lesson, which is a good thing because I'm way more distracted than I should be. I keep thinking about Finn and the proposal and Maxon. I haven't made any decisions, but I still feel like I'm hurtling toward the finish line.

Whether I want to be or not.

"Okay," I call to the twins at last. They're circling their ponies at the other end of the arena and doing a great job of listening and being careful. "Let's bring them to the center and you can tell me what your favorite parts of today were."

Smiles stretch across their faces. They always love this part—so do I. It puts the emphasis on the positive, and right now, I feel like I could use that even more than they could.

"What was your favorite part today?" I ask Bridget, holding Drama's reins so she can dismount. The little girl kicks free of the saddle and drops neatly to the ground.

"Galloping!" she says, beaming.

I laugh. "That was cantering, but yes." I turn to Al Capony, taking the pony's reins for Brody. "What about you, buddy?"

"The galloping," he says. "Because my cantering really was galloping because Al is way faster than Drama."

"No, he isn't!"

"Yes, he is!"

"Enough!" Parker shouts. She's laughing, but the kids still knock it off. I gotta admit, it's impressive. She strides ahead, keeping one hand on Bridget and one hand on Drama as we walk back to the stable.

"Miss Libby?"

"Yeah?" I look down at Brody and his little face is screwed up with worry.

"Are you okay?" he whispers.

I hesitate. "I've...been better. I'm sorry, buddy. Did I seem distracted?"

"No. The lesson was fun. I can just tell you're sad."

And that shouldn't make me sadder, but it does. I ruffle his hair. "I'll have to perk up then."

"Who made you sad?"

I hesitate again. I don't want to lie, but it's not like he needs to know the full truth either. "I had a fight with a friend," I say at last.

"Oh." Brody's tone changes from worried little boy into worldly little old man. He nods. "A friend. When Parker and Aiden were friends they would fight and it made them really sad too. Now they're boyfriend and girlfriend though and they don't fight as much—or if they do, they make up really quickly." He turns to me, face bright. "Hey, want to know what I learned?"

Oh, boy. There's almost no telling what Brody could mean here. How to superglue a toilet shut? How to stick Crayons under his uncle's windshield wipers so when he turned them on a rainbow smeared across the glass? Because I saw that one personally and Aiden and Brody had to scrub the windshield for a good hour before everything came up.

"Tell me," I say at last, crossing my fingers it isn't anything gross. "What did you learn?"

"That sorry doesn't always mean sorry. It only means sorry if you change the way you act."

"That's...very true."

Brody nods. "I know. Like this morning, when I cut off Bridget's Barbie's ponytail? I said I was sorry, but if I get another chance to do it, I'm gonna do it. Some bad things are too satisfying not to do again."

I'm pretty sure this is the part where I should scold him, but I can't bring myself to do it. He's right. Some bad things are too much fun not to do again.

"You ready?" Parker asks Brody, coming out of the stable with Bridget at her side. Parker looks amazing as always in her tall Frye boots and skinny jeans, but Bridget has hay in her hair and a smudge of dirt on her nose. She also looks completely happy and content with life. It makes me smile. Some kids just really blossom with horses around. These two certainly have.

"Yeah, I'm ready to go," Brody says, stubbing the toe of his boot into the gravel. "If we have to."

"Let me guess, you'd rather clean stalls than clean your room?" Parker asks, trying to fight down a smile.

Brody's eyes go wide. "Is that an option? Can we?"

"You kill me, kid. You know that?"

"I try."

It's one of those silly, throwaway exchanges, but somehow Parker and Brody manage to pack so much love and fondness into it. "You're not getting out of cleaning your room," she tells him. "Thanks for the lesson, Libby. I left the money on the tack room desk."

"Great!"

Parker and Bridget leave and Brody tugs my hand, pulling me down to his level. His cheeks are pink from the wind and his blond hair sticks out in all directions. "Can I tell you a secret, Libby?"

"Of course."

"I love Parker, but sometimes really miss my mom. I wish she could see me ride."

My heart squeezes. From what I understand, the twins' mother is somewhere abroad. Her current boyfriend didn't want the kids so she packed them off to their grandmother who packed them off to Aiden. Aiden and Parker have been the only steady things in the kids' lives for ages now.

I give him a hug. "I know you miss her, honey. I hope one day she can see you ride too."

"I hope so too." He hesitates. "You think she will?"

"Gosh, I hope so." And briefly I feel kind of sick. Brody missing his mom makes me think of Finn all over again. He lost his too. We love our moms so much. I don't know what I would do if I lost mine.

Now my heart's squeezing all over again. Finn never had the family I have—or that the twins now have.

We'll have to make our own family, I think.

"I hope she'll come too." His expression brightens and he turns for the Jeep. "See you soon!"

I grin. "Hey, Brody?"

"Yeah?"

"Leave Bridget's Barbies alone."

He narrows his eyes and spins around, stomping off in a huff. Parker helps him into the Jeep and then waves to me. "See you next week!"

"Absolutely!"

I watch them drive off. It's cold and I should go in, but I can't seem get myself to move. Brody's observation, "sorry doesn't always mean sorry. It only means sorry if you change the way you act," is on loop in my head. It makes me think about my actions.

But it really makes me think about Finn's.

He's been all in.

We could go public, I realize. We should go public. He isn't the Finn he was before—and I'm not the same Libby. We've grown.

His apology was genuine. Going public with me isn't a 'fuck you,' it was proving to me that he was all in. It wasn't a grand gesture like when he rented out the Fox—even though it was in its own way—it was the only gesture he wanted to make. He wanted us to be together.

The realization swoops my stomach into my feet. We'll have to make our own family.

And that's when I discover I've had my answer all along: Yes, I will marry him.

"But I told him I wouldn't," I whisper, my stomach sinking even lower and then I hear the crunch of tires on gravel and I know even before I turn that it's Finn.

That I'm going to have to make this right.

CHAPTER 35 | Finn

I glimpse Libby standing by the stable doors as I pull in. The wind whips dark tendrils of hair from her braid and her face is pale. From the cold or from me? Her parents told me to try again, but what if it's too late?

The idea almost makes me laugh. It would be fitting, wouldn't it? Our whole relationship has been the definition of 'too late': I told her the truth too late. I told her how I feel too late.

Our history is our destiny.

I park, and for several seconds, I can't breathe. The sky feels like it's lowering and I know a panic attack is coming on. Everything's coming to a head: my dad, Libby's parents, my fucking failed proposal, Libby doubting me.

She's never doubted me. Ever. Until I bared everything I am to ask her to marry me.

I inhale once, again. I kick open my car door and chill wind snakes inside, bracing me. I get out and make my way toward the stable. Libby's still by the arched entrance, eyes huge and cheeks pale. She looks a little anxious, enormously beautiful...

And like everything I've ever wanted.

"Finn, I—"

"I got my head straight." I walk straight to her and she backs up. For a second, I'm thrown. Is she scared? Pulling away?

And then her hands go to her scarf and she tugs it loose. She isn't backing away from me, she's drawing me closer and I can't help but follow.

"I was wrong about what I said earlier," she tells me, eyes pinned to mine. She reaches the tack room door and opens it, taking us both inside. "I was out of line."

"You weren't. I—"

"I don't want to talk about it. I'm just so glad you came home."

Home. I have about a nanosecond to register the word before she's yanking me down to her, fitting her mouth over mine. I've always loved kissing Libby, but this is a whole new level of perfect. Her tongue finds mine. Her body fits against me.

I bend to pick her up and she leaps into my arms. "I thought we were over," she whispers and it damn near shatters what's left of me.

"I've never been over you." It comes out rough like I've dredged it up from some place hidden. "I could never be over you."

"Then show me."

Fucking gladly. I start toward her desk and she shakes her head. "Upstairs. I want all of you."

It strikes me stupid. I barely realize I'm carrying her up to the apartment. I barely notice striding through her kitchen. Some long-buried memory from when we were kids surfaces and I remember the apartment's bedroom is off to the left and I head that way.

"On the bed," Libby orders as I push through her bedroom door. "Put me on the bed and watch me while I undress for you."

My hard-on—already aching—throbs. I toss her down, trying to channel some of our usual teasing and laughing, but Libby's whole body is strung tight. She arches back into the covers, making quick work of her clothes and revealing the curves that can take me to my knees.

"Do you like this?" she whispers, pulling off her sweater and exposing bare skin and barely contained breasts. "Finn?"

I can't answer. I can barely breathe. She looks so perfect lying there and I'm supposed to form words?

She grins. "Speechless is a good look for you." Her hands slide up the insides of her thighs, parting them for me. Her eyes drop to my hard-on and she licks her lips. "Please."

I groan, tugging my shirt over my head with suddenly clumsy fingers.

"Let me," Libby says, scrambling to me. "I want to do it."

And I want it done fast and now, but I wait. I let her, trying not to groan again when she runs her soft palms down my bare chest to my stomach to my belt buckle. She stares into my eyes, smiling wickedly as she undoes it.

My hard-on springs free and she takes me with both hands, rubbing me up and down. "I never get tired of him," she breathes.

And that's all I can take, I think and kick out of my boots, drop my pants and my boxers. She gives me another wicked smile and pulls my hips to her, pulls me until I'm on top and my weight must be damn near crushing her and she still can't seem to get enough.

"Show me how you could never be over me," she whispers against the corner of my mouth. "Show me."

Fucking gladly. I thrust against her once, sliding my length against her heat and making her moan. I kiss down her body, enjoying her curves, her softness. She feels like fucking heaven, like everything I need right now.

Like everything I'll ever need.

"Please, Finn, please," she pants, legs falling wide for me. She's so damn beautiful it stops me dead. I could look at her like this all day and then she whispers, "Please."

And I unravel.

I pin her down. I worship her with my mouth like she loves and I crave. I lick circles around her clit, sucking it softly into my mouth and then blowing gently across her. Every stroke takes her higher.

And then I hold her there.

"Yesyesyes! Pleasepleaseplease!" Her head thrashes back and forth against her pillow, desperate. I love her like this.

I love her.

I kiss the inside of her thigh and set in again, licking firmer and firmer circles around her clit and easing one finger inside her...and then two. She goes even wetter for me, riding my fingers and my mouth. This is for her, but I can't help but enjoy it too. The way she moves. The way she *moans*.

She spreads her thighs even wider, frantic to come. I pull back a bit, blowing across her swollen clit again and making her hips jump. It earns me another moan—this one caught between frustration and delight.

"Finn—"

And then I fuck her with my tongue.

She cries out, grinding down on me and grabbing my hair. Her frantic hands and even more frantic gasps damn near cripple me. My dick aches for her. My balls are throbbing.

But I keep going. I adore her pussy until her head's thrown back again, until she's wild against my mouth.

Until she understands I'm sorry and I could never walk away from her and she's my only.

"Finn! I-I'm coming!" And then she's gone. All her words swallowed up by the pleasure. I get to watch how her back arches, how her hips lift. Tremors shake her body and she screams my name over and over again, wrenching me closer so I can tongue every aftershock from her, kiss every shudder.

She goes boneless, shuddery, and I finally pull back. Look up to see how she's shaking in my hands, eyes gone huge.

Like I've shattered her

Which would be about damn appropriate. I feel the same way. I run my thumbs along the tender skin of her inner thighs. "Libs?"

"I love you," she whispers, sounding lost. "For always."

CHAPTER 36 | Libby

"I love you for always," I whisper and it might be the truest thing I've ever said. The truest thing I've ever known.

I look down at Finn, meeting his heated gaze. His mouth is wet from me and his hands grip me like I belong to him.

And I do. Heart, body, and soul.

"I love you too," he whispers, but his expression is watchful, like he's afraid I'm about to take it back.

That'll come, I think, reaching for him. With enough time, he'll realize I'm not leaving. Ever.

My hand grazes his cheek and suddenly he's leaning over me, kissing me hard until all I can feel is Finn and all I can taste is us. When he fucked me with his tongue, it blew me apart. I could feel his worship, his love, his desire. It was everything.

But I can already feel my body wanting more.

We break apart, gasping and I cup his face with both hands. "There's nothing you can do to scare me away," I whisper, holding my gaze to his. I can't tell what he's thinking. Heat and desire and want are twisted with uncertainty and love. "I'm all in. Are you?"

"Always. Forever."

And then he enters me with a dizzying thrust. I arch against him, delighting in the fullness and friction, and he takes me to the hilt, rubbing my tender clit so I gasp.

So I want more.

He pulls back and slides in again, setting a rhythm that makes my toes curl and my eyes slide shut.

I tighten my legs around him, enjoying the closeness and the fullness. He strokes me once, again. Need coils deep inside me. He's so hard and so long. Every thrust rubs that secret place inside me that takes me dizzyingly high.

"You feel so good," I moan. "I want more."

"I always want more," he says, punctuating the words with another stroke. He circles his hips and I arch against him. "I can't get enough of you. Your ass, your breasts, your perfect fucking pussy."

Another circle and lock my ankles behind him. It pulls him close and pleasure sparks through me, spinning the world around me.

"I can't get enough of you," he growls into my ear, one hand sliding between us to tease me more. It drives me straight to that cliff, straight to that point of no-return, and he knows it. His eyes never leave mine as he taps me once, twice, sparking

I can feel him everywhere, I think.

And then I shatter.

Pleasure rips through me, turning the room hazy and distant. I'm screaming his name and it should be impossible but I can somehow hear him whisper mine.

"Look at me, Libs," he breathes and I do. His gorgeous face is inches from mine and his eyes are drinking me in. It feels like there will be nothing left when he's done.

"You're so beautiful," he whispers, gentling his strokes so he's riding my aftershocks and making me gasp. His hands frame my face and I lean my cheek into his palm, opening my eyes to look up at him. He's beautiful and wounded and mine.

And I'm his.

"Come for me," he breathes, thrusting his hips and treating me to a brain-scrambling kiss. "Come for me again."

"I can't."

But then he strokes me again and I realize I can. His grip, his strokes, *him*. It all turns my joints to liquid, turns my body boneless.

And then he flips us and I'm straddling him. His hands go to my hips and he lifts me up and then brings me down. "Look at you," he grates, bouncing me in that way that always *always* makes me gasp. "Look at you."

I do. I'm completely naked, completely exposed. Sunlight from the window streams over us and there's nowhere to hide anything—and I feel even sexier because of it.

"You like me on top," I say, grinning.

"I like you every which way." And then he bounces me again. I moan. The friction, the heat, they're driving us both to an edge that feels familiar and unknown all at the same time.

"Again," he commands and strokes me faster, harder. Every thrust takes me higher, promising a release even more power than before. My head lolls back, my whole body relaxing into the pleasure he's giving me.

"You're fucking perfect, Libby."

And it pushes me over once more.

I feel like I fall out of orbit, like I'm ripped away until to a place where there's only Finn and only his touch. Dimly, I can hear him groaning my name. I slump, completely exhausted, and he eases me into him.

For several moments, all I can do is pant and stare at the ceiling. What we have...what just happened between us...it feels like so much more than it ever was before—not that sex with Finn hasn't always been mind-shattering, not that he hasn't left me panting before, but this feels...

Like making love, I realize. We made love for the first time. It wasn't just sex. It was connection.

I snuggle into him and his fingertips drift up my spine, trailing stars across my skin. "So I guess you accept my apology?"

I laugh. "Only if you accept mine."

"Goes without saying." He turns to me, his expression incredibly tender. "I want you to know Maxon won't be a problem for us. I took care of it."

The tiniest fissure of alarm threads through me. "How?"

"I confronted him. We have him dead to rights. This is over—even if he doesn't think it is."

I stiffen. "Finn, he isn't going to let you go. Look what he did to keep you, the lies he told, the people he ruined."

"Yes, look at them." He shifts so we're fully face-to-face and his hard chest feels so reassuring and real under my palms. "Thanks to Carol, I can bring all of that to light and he knows it. Maxon's many things, but he isn't suicidal."

I hesitate. "Can you really leave this thing between you two?"

"For you. Absolutely." It's so quick it should be a line or a lie, but it isn't. Somehow I know that. Maybe because this is Finn and this is me and this is...us.

Maybe your history isn't your destiny, I think—and then realize maybe it is. Because all those years ago, we'd confessed how we were in love with each other and here we are, today, still in love. Even more in love.

He strokes his fingertips across my cheek. "One more thing though. I need to ask you..."

My heart leaps. "Yes?"

"Be my date to the holiday party?"

Oh. For a second, I'm in free-fall. I thought he was going to propose again, but I button-on a smile. "I'd love to," I say and it's the truth. I want nothing more than to take our relationship into the light. No more sneaking around. No more lying. We can be together and figure out what 'together' means.

I sit up, grinning. "I'll have to go shopping for a dress."

"Good. I'll come with you."

"You want to go shopping with me? Sit there while I try on a bazillion dresses and probably hate them all?"

He grins. "Absolutely. Because then I'll get to help you take them off."

And then he kisses me again.

CHAPTER 37 | Libby

Finn wasn't kidding when he said the holiday party was seriously themed-out. The Ritz-Carlton's ballroom has been redecorated to look like a vintage carnival. There are games and food carts lining the far walls, a violin quartet playing Fall Out Boy and U2 covers, and up above, the ballroom's ceiling is covered in a million tiny white lights, like every star in the universe is twinkling down on us.

Honestly, I could stand here all night, enjoying them, but I'm on the move, looking for the girls and Finn.

And, well, avoiding the carnival clowns.

An orange-haired one starts to wander my way and I hold up one finger. "Ah ah," I tell him and his wide, red mouth stretches into a crazy, *creepy* smile. "No hugs."

The crazy smile turns upside down and now it's a comical—and still creepy—frown.

"I don't care," I continue. "No one likes clowns and you know it."

His eyes go wide. "Hey!"

"Libby!" Ally bounces up to my side, looking drop-dead gorgeous in a slinky white dress and a top hat. She's tilted it to the side so she looks like a jaunty ring leader and her grin is practically wrapped around her head. "Have you tried the funnel cakes? They're amazing!"

The orange-haired clown's eyes go bright and he starts edging toward Ally, no doubt fully intending to give her a bear-hug.

Without looking away from me, she jams one finger in his direction. "Don't you dare." The clown's shoulders slump and Ally ignores him. "Seriously. You should try it." And then she jams a bunch of fried dough dusted in powdered sugar into my mouth.

So now I'm pretty much laughing, choking, and chewing. She's right. It is, in fact, amazing. "Yeah, I'm going to need more of that," I say at last, swallowing.

"I know, right? Laurel's bringing more back. I say we eat ourselves into a sugar coma."

I laugh. "Some of us are working tonight, remember? I'm supposed to be here as Oliver Holdings' charity work."

Ally takes a huge bite of funnel cake and looks over my dress. It's a strapless Stella McCartney. Finn and I picked it out together—and then he nearly jumped me in the dressing room when he saw me in it. "Yeah, you totally look like a charity case," she says, grinning. "Like the sexiest charity case ever."

"I didn't say charity 'case.' I said charity *work* and give me that." We play fight over the last bit of funnel cake and I win. I pop it into my mouth and chew. "Ugh. That's really good. I hope Laurel gets here soon."

"Where's Finn?" Ally asks.

"I haven't seen him yet." I take a sip of my champagne and try to ignore the butterflies in my stomach. I drove in with the girls—we got ready together and everything, it was so much fun, like doing prom in high school all over again. Finn was stuck at the office and was going to meet me here. "I hope he likes the dress," I add, running a hand over the draped silk.

Ally laughs. "Pretty sure he liked the dress if he tried to jump you in the store."

I blush. Maybe there are some things I shouldn't tell my friends, but for the past several weeks, things with Finn have been all kinds of perfect and I can't help gushing. Or sharing too much information. It's a fine line for me, I guess. "Yeah," I say, "but he hasn't seen the whole thing together. I have makeup on, my hair's not a wreck, my—"

"Nerves are getting the best of me," Ally finishes.

"Yeah, fine, but not for the reason you think." She quirks one brow and I hurry to finish: "I'm not scared of everyone knowing we're together. I'm scared of screwing up in front of his coworkers. What if I say the wrong thing?"

"What is she worrying about?" Laurel joins us, a plate of funnel cakes in each hand. She passes one to Ally and looks at me. "This is your night. You'll feel better once he's here and the whole check ceremony thing is over."

"Yeah, good point." I take another sip of champagne and notice another clown—a blue-haired one this time—headed our way. "Ugh. We have company."

"Yes, we do," Ally says, but she's looking the other direction and I can tell by the amusement in her voice, it's Finn.

I turn, spotting him right away. He's easily a half a head taller than everyone else and gorgeous. His black tuxedo clings to his hard lines perfectly, his dark hair is slightly mussed—like he's been running his hands through it—and his jaw is set.

Until he sees me and his whole expression relaxes.

He smiles and my heart swings like a pendant on a string.

"You two are ridiculous," Ally says, laughing.

"He's almost...pretty," Laurel adds. She tilts her head to one side, studying him as he approaches. I think it over, trying to see Finn as they're seeing him and deciding...they're kinda right. He's the sort of beautiful that makes women—and men—stare.

And he's coming for me.

"Dance with me," Ally announces. She grabs Laurel's hand and pulls her toward the dance floor. "They have to work, but we get to party!"

The girls grin before ducking into the crowd and leaving me to Finn. He waves and they wave back and then suddenly he's toe-to-toe with me and my whole world is made up of him.

"Hi," I breathe.

"Hi, you look amazing," he says, eyes raking up and down me and my skin going hot.

"I feel amazing when you look at me like that."

"Really?" He grins. "I didn't know that."

"Yep. It's true." I lick my lower lip and taste powdered sugar. The violin quartet finishes up U2's With Or Without You and starts in on Fall Out Boy's "Thnks fr th Mmrs."

"It's like a superpower," I continue, my pulse beginning to climb. "You look at me like that and I feel like I can conquer the world." I drop my voice to a whisper: "You look at me like that and I get wet."

He groans and steps closer.

So I step back. I draw both of us into the shadows. "I love you, you know that?"

Finn's grin goes silvery from the lights. "I do—but I never get tired of hearing it."

"I love you," I repeat. My shoulders hit the wall behind me and his hands go to either side of my face, holding me like I'm precious.

He leans in, mouth brushing mine. "I love you too. More than anything. I can't believe we got a second chance at this."

"I can't either. I'm so grateful." And I am. Silly maybe, but true. "There were so many things keeping us apart and yet we kept finding our way back to each other. How lucky are we?"

"Dunno. Maybe we should find out?" Finn shifts, his hand going into his tuxedo jacket pocket and emerging with a diamond ring. Even the shadows can't hide its sparkle.

Or size.

Oh. My. God.

"Marry me?" he whispers, bringing me back.

I swallow. "Finn...that ring is huge."

"I can't tell if that's a yes." His voice is wry, amused—but there's a touch of uncertainty snaking underneath and it makes my throat catch.

"Of course, it's a yes!" I hug him hard and he hugs me back. For several seconds, we just hold each other. "Yes," I repeat, finally breaking apart. "Yes, I will marry you!"

I place one hand against his cheek, trying to memorize this moment. "Do you know once I thought our history was our destiny? That we were fated to fail because we'd failed before?"

A strange light comes into his eyes. Recognition? Hurt?

It's both, I realize.

"I felt the same way, Libs, but it isn't like that at all. Our destiny is going to be what we make it. Together."

I smile. "Forever."

Want to see how Finn and Libby started it all?

Sign up[1] for a FREE prequel novella and get notified about Emma Ashe book releases, cover reveals, and bonus material!

...

Get the next book: **emmaashe.com/books[2]**

...

Read on for an excerpt from *Deeper Than Lies*, Book #2 in the Deeper Than Love Series

---

1. http://www.emmaashe.com/signup-book

2. http://www.emmaashe.com/books/deeper

TEASER CHAPTER 1 | Ellie

So that's *Hot Stuff*?! I crane my head, trying—and failing—to see across the crowded dance floor. It's too dark to see much. I mean, I can tell he's big. The guy is at least a head taller than anyone else in here, but *hot*? Gag me. He's my sister's fiancé, which means I don't need to know if he's hot.

I need to know if he's a cheater.

"You know your glare can't actually set him on fire, right?" The club is so noisy Holly has to lean close. Her breath is hot in my ear.

I scowl. "Maybe I can. Maybe I've been secretly developing laser eyes."

My best friend laughs. "When it comes to Wren, I would believe it." She hooks her arm through mine, sipping on a neon-colored drink as we watch my beloved older sister touch Hot Stuff's arm. They laugh.

"She looks really happy, Ellie."

"Wren's always happy," I say, sipping my own neon-colored drink. It's too sweet and turns my mouth sticky. "And then they cheat on her and she's devastated. I love my sister, but we have crappy taste in men. We can't help it. It's genetic."

Holly faces me. The disco lights have turned her pale hair green and red. Her blue eyes look electric. "Please don't do this."

"I have to."

"No, you don't. If it works, you're the woman who kissed her sister's fiancé. If it doesn't work, you're the woman who *tried* to kiss her sister's fiancé."

"Gross!" The idea of kissing my sister's fiancé is worse than my overly sweet drink. I nearly gag. "I'm not going to kiss him! That's horrible!"

"Then what—"

183

"I'm just going to get chatty. Flirt a little. Make sure he tells me he has a fiancée and she's beautiful and brilliant, like a good guy would. If I have to, I'll invite him to leave with me, and if he gives me his number, we'll know he's an ass."

"Or." Holly holds up one finger. "You could wait and get to know him."

I glare at Holly because she's right and also because we've been over this. Technically, the guy's name isn't Hot Stuff. It's Tate Matthews. But ever since I read this text where Wren called him Hot Stuff, I can't get it out of my mind. I mean *really*. Hot. Stuff. Ugh.

Anyway, Wren met him while visiting her mom's family in Paris. She does this every summer and she always tells me everything. Except this time, she dated the guy for two months before even mentioning him. Then they spent all last month living together, and *now* they're saying "I love you," giving out nicknames, and getting *married*. I've never even met him.

Hot Stuff flew in this afternoon to visit and Wren picked him up from the airport. They decided to celebrate his arrival with dinner and dancing and I was supposed to come, but I got stuck at the farm—which turned out to be a huge blessing because *now* he doesn't know what I look like. I mean, sure, he could've Facebook stalked me or whatever, but thanks to my crazy work hours I can't remember the last time someone took a picture of me that didn't involve sweaty ponytails and riding breeches. Cleaned up, I look way different. *Now*, I can ambush him and find out if he's horn dog cheater.

"It's like the universe planned this," I mutter.

"What?"

"Nothing." It's a great idea—it *is*—and yet my stomach is in knots. I take a deep breath. "Sometimes you have to do something terrible to do something right."

"That doesn't even make sense."

"Yes, it does. Look, Holls, you know how hard Wren took her last break up. She's getting *married* to this guy. I've never seen her so in love. If he turns out to be a troll, she'll be devastated. Remember Brian the Super Jerk?"

Holly nods grimly. "And Craig from her freshman bio class."

"And James the gigantic tool."

"James was *your* gigantic tool, not Wren's."

I blink, flashing back to a six feet plus of dark hair, darker eyes, and a pair of fast hands. Not coincidentally, the last fast hands that have touched me in almost a year. "You're right," I say at last. "But I think my point is still made. Wren and I cannot be trusted to pick out boyfriends, let alone husbands, and—"

"And I want to know where my uptight friend has gone. Even if you're not going to touch him, you're still inviting him to leave with you."

"If he leaves with some girl who offers him a go in the parking lot, he doesn't deserve my sister."

Holly goes quiet, and I know she agrees. "This isn't like you," she says at last. She's right too. Outside the club, I'm a respected profession-al rider. I have clients, sale horses, a *business*. I might only be twenty-three, but I have goals, and I'm usually not prone to dramatics.

But I'm also not prone to discovering my sister is about to get mar-ried to a guy I've never met, and run off to New York, and leave every-one we love behind, and—

Get it together, I tell myself. I grab Holly's hand and squeeze. "You love Wren as much as I do. Help me make sure she's going to be happy with that idiot."

"That 'idiot' could be your brother in law. Do you really want to mess this up?"

"No, but I would rather Hot Stuff be mad at me for the rest of our lives than see Wren heartbroken. Please, Holly?" After a ridiculously long moment, she sighs, and I know I have her. I grin. "You're the best, you know that?"

Holly rolls her eyes, and we watch Wren and Hot Stuff share another laugh over something he said. The DJ fires up another remix of some Top 40 Hit, and the crowd cheers. More people rush to the dance floor, someone jostling me as she passes.

I barely notice. Wren is patting Hot Stuff's forearm, telling him something. She moves away, purse in hand. I push up on my tip-toes trying to see better. Is she going to the bathroom? For another drink? It doesn't matter, I guess. Hot Stuff is alone now and my opportunity is here.

I adjust my already low cut dress until my breasts are on the verge of exploding. "Okay." I turn to Holly. "How do I look?"

"Like a crazy woman with weird tan lines."

I scowl again and peer at my shoulders. She's right. Thanks to spending most of yesterday afternoon working on the pasture fencing, pale lines from my tank top crisscross my skin. "Ugh, I'd hoped you wouldn't be able to see them."

"You can't. Not really." Holly rubs her forehead like I've given her a headache. I probably have. "You're still crazy though."

Sadly, she's absolutely right. "Sometimes you have to do crazy stuff to protect the people you love," I tell her. "Wren will forgive me...eventually." The thought makes my stomach squeeze again. "Hold my drink?"

Holly eyes the half-finished peach martini. "How many of these have you had?"

"Three?"

"And when did you get your brilliant idea?"

"Sometime around the second. I'm not drunk though. I know what I'm doing. I *do*. I'm going to flirt with him, maybe invite him outside, and if he says 'yes' I'll out him for the ass he is. It's a good plan. It'll work."

Holly opens her mouth and then shuts it. "Good luck," she says at last.

I nod and totter across the dance floor, needing four or five strides before I get my balance. I love heels, but I spend most of my time in boots, and it shows. I probably look like a five-year-old wearing her mommy's shoes.

To compensate, I stick my chest out. *You can do this. You can do this.*

Four feet away though I'm suddenly not so sure. Hot Stuff turns and the strobe lights catch his face: full lips, high cheekbones, and a hard edged jaw. He's wearing dark jeans, and a black dress shirt, the tails untucked and the top buttons undone. Hot Stuff is indeed hot. So hot, in fact, I forget I'm staring—with my mouth open—until he smiles.

"Hey, there."

Oh, God and he has a southern accent. Wren really does have amazing taste in jerks.

So do you, I remind myself, snapping my mouth shut and matching Hot Stuff's smile. "Hey, yourself. Are you having a good time?"

"Better now."

Jerk Alert bells go off in my head and any doubt I had about my plan vanishes. He's having a better time now that my sister isn't here? He's an ass.

I'm so *going to take you down*, I think, widening my smile and shimmying closer. His gaze briefly dips, taking in my cleavage and the form fitting dress, and now I hate him even more.

"Do you live around here?" I ask.

He shrugs. "Just moved back."

"Lucky me."

A smile tugs at one corner of Hot Stuff's mouth and, again, I see what Wren sees in him. He's pretty. I know you're not supposed to call guys that, but he is.

I ease a little closer. "So where'd you move from?"

"Ireland."

"Wow!" For a second, my sexy girl coming onto him thing slips and the real me shows through. I can't help it. I've always wanted to go to Ireland. Some of the best show jumping riders in the world have trained there.

Focus, Ellie! "Wow," I repeat, sounding a little more like the drunken party girl I'm supposed to be. "That's really far away."

"Not nearly far enough."

Oh. Well, okay then. Hot Stuff has gone from flirty to broody. He glares out at the dancers like they have personally offended him. I slide another step closer though and his attention snaps back to me. It's probably a trick of the light, but his expression seems to soften.

Not. Good. "So what brings you to Atlanta?" I ask. *You better say my sister*, I think.

Hot Stuff frowns. "Work. I'm applying for a manager position."

Hmm, he didn't mention Wren, but he isn't exactly flirting anymore either. For several seconds, we stare at each other.

"Are *you* local?" Hot Stuff asks. "What do you do for fun?"

Fun? What's that? I train horses and when I'm not training horses I'm thinking about training horses. Until tonight, I couldn't have even told you where this club was, but I could tell you the location of four tack shops, six breeding farms, and about a dozen stables. I like to think it's because I know my market. Wren says it's because I'm not well rounded.

"Oh, I don't know," I say at last, making a show of playing with my hair. It needs a cut and the overlong ends brush past my elbows. "I guess it depends on the person you're with."

The half-smile turns into a full-fledged grin, and my stomach sinks. My poor sister. He's a cheater.

"Yeah?" Hot Stuff asks.

"Yeah." I take a deep—*deep*—breath and force my hand to cup his arm. The muscles beneath my palm tighten. "I mean, we could stay here and have fun...or we could go somewhere else..." I trail off, hoping innuendo will be enough. I don't have a ton of experience with sexy stuff. Okay, I have almost no experience with sexy stuff. Work doesn't leave me a lot of free time, and it seems like every guy I date turns into a huge jerk.

Hot Stuff's left eyebrow raises. "Somewhere else?"

Ugh. Think. I shift from foot to foot and wobble, hip bumping into the glossy-topped table.

Hot Stuff puts one hand on my arm, gently squeezing. "Are you okay?"

I don't think so. I blink, blink again. The floor feels like it's tilting under my feet, and that wobble definitely wasn't from the heels. Maybe I am drunk?

Maybe this *is* a bad idea.

"Do you need me to get you a cab?" he asks.

I lift my face to tell him I'm fine, and realize we're inches apart. I'm close enough to smell the bourbon on his breath, close enough...to kiss.

Run! Except I can't because Hot Stuff's hand has suddenly found my wrist. I can feel the heat of him. He comes closer...closer...

"Ellie?"

My stomach lurches. Wren. I spin around and see my big sister standing only a few feet away. She has a drink in each hand and looks like she's biting down a laugh.

I launch myself away from Hot Stuff. "He's a cheater, Wren! He was going to kiss me!"

"Cheater?" Wren puts the drinks on a hip high table and trots to my side. She presses a cool hand to my head like she did when I was little and sick with the flu. "Honey, Caleb's single. Are you feeling okay?"

"No, I'm fine—wait. *What?* I thought you said his name was Tate."

Wren cocks her head, her smooth brown ponytail slipping down one shoulder. "No. *That's* Caleb." She motions to the guy beside me before turning in the direction of another. One who could also be called hot.

Oh, crap.

"*That's* Tate," she says, hands going to her hips. "Caleb was about to kiss you."

TEASER CHAPTER 2 | Caleb

What the hell? The pretty brunette takes another wobbly step away from me and squares her shoulders. She looks from Tate to me and back to Tate.

"Nice to meet you," she says at last and offers him a hand. "I'm Ellie, Wren's sister."

Tate and Ellie shake like this is completely normal and she wasn't just flirting with *me* because she thought I was *him*.

I don't even know where to begin with this shit and it looks like Wren agrees. Eyes narrowed, she glares at her sister. "What's going on?"

Ellie chews her lower lip for a long moment, no doubt searching for something to say that won't sound crazy.

Newsflash, sweetheart, you are *crazy.* I lean one arm against the tabletop, and give Tate a sympathetic look. *See what you're marrying into, buddy.*

Tate won't meet my eyes, but he scratches his temple with his middle finger in response.

Fine. Your funeral. He may not have had his fill of party girls and their games, but I have. I barely escaped Mandy. I may be home again, but I'm not going back for another round of crazy. In fact, I can't believe I almost fell for it again. Or maybe I can. When it comes to women, I have terrible taste. If she's a beautiful party girl prone to bad decisions, she's the girl for me.

Or she was, like I said I've had my fill of crazy.

"OhmygodWren!" Another girl shoulders her way out of the dance floor and into our group. She's curvy and pale-haired and moves like she could run a mile in those four-inch heels. "It's not what you think!"

"Holly?" Wren glances from her sister to the Holly girl, corners of her mouth turned down. "What are you doing here?"

"Uh," Holly manages. Her eyes are huge and guilty. "I came with Ellie."

Ah, the partner in crime. Crazy always travels in packs. I'm going to need more booze to handle this. I start looking for our waitress. Unfortunately for me, there's no sign of her. The club is way crowded, and someone is breaking out glow sticks, the universal promise of bad decisions to come.

"Why are you here? You guys said you couldn't come—are you *spying* on me?" Wren's voice skews higher and I wince. Wren's a nice girl. When Tate introduced us, I never expected to like her as much as I do. She doesn't deserve whatever stupidity her sister and friend have cooked up.

"Of course I'm not spying on you!" Ellie starts toward Wren and then pauses, thinking hard. She's definitely drunk. I wasn't entirely sure earlier, but there's no mistaking the glassy, overbright eyes and the sway to her step now. "Okay, it's a little like spying, but not like you think. I was never going to kiss him. I was just going to flirt with him so we'd know if he was an ass."

Oh, there's some logic for you. Our waitress squeezes a group of guys blocking the tables, and I catch her eye, signaling for another drink. If only there were a universal hand sign for keep-them-coming-until-I-pass-out. Normally, I would just leave, but Wren's my ride, and at this rate, we're not getting out of here any time soon. I predict tears with a side of screaming.

Actually...I eye Wren. She's drawing herself up to her full height—all barely five and a half feet of her—and both her hands are clenched. Actually, it may be screaming with a side of tears. If she starts throwing punches, I will be impressed.

And not really surprised because insanity runs in families and clearly the Ellie girl has issues.

"Look, Wren." Ellie reaches for her sister's arm and Wren pulls away. "I can explain."

"No," Holly says, wide-eyed. She steps between the sisters and wraps one arm around Wren's shoulders. "*You* stay put," she says to Ellie. "*I* will explain."

Holly pulls Wren and Tate away as the waitress returns with my bourbon. "Thank you," I say and pass her a ten.

Her face lights up. "Sure thing, honey."

"Keep them coming," I say, shaking the glass. She nods and disappears into the thickening crowd. The night is definitely heating up. People are flinging themselves around on the dance floor and pounding back drinks at the bar. Maybe a dozen feet away, a gorgeous girl with waist-length dark hair and a wicked pair of legs twines herself around a guy who holds her like she is his everything.

I used to look at Mandy like that, I think, and it feels like a kick to the gut.

"Well, this is awkward."

I glance down, bourbon almost to my lips. Ellie is now standing by my side. She chews the skin next to her thumb, watching Holly talk to Wren and Tate. Whatever Holly's saying, they don't seem to be impressed. Actually, Tate seems kind of horrified. He's standing even straighter than usual and staring down at Holly with that calculating expression he usually reserves for the courtroom.

I turn back to Ellie. "You thought I was Tate? What was that? Some sort of game?"

Wren's sister glares at me and crosses her arms. Moments ago, I would've said that was to better highlight her assets, but now I think it's just because she's pissed. I honestly don't think Ellie realizes how close she is to popping out of that dress—or how hard I'm struggling not to look at her almost popping out of that dress.

"It was...an experiment," she finally manages.

"An experiment?" That makes zero sense. I eye her. "How drunk are you?"

"Not nearly enough." Ellie looks up at me through a fringe of bangs and even though I know she's a drama queen and I can't stand drama queens, those big, brown eyes hit something low in my gut. "I owe you an apology," she continues. "I was being...stupid."

"No kidding." Okay, I could've been more gracious, but I'm still annoyed. Freaking party girls.

Ellie forces her shoulders back. "Okay, I deserved that. Can we try again? I'm Ellie."

She offers me her hand and I finish my bourbon in one quick swallow. Her palm is surprisingly cool against mine. "Caleb."

"How do you know Tate?"

"I'm his best friend."

At least she has the good grace to wince. We spend another uncomfortable moment watching Tate, Wren, and Holly talking. Holly points at Ellie and then twirls one finger around her temple in the universal symbol for crazy. Everyone nods and Ellie huffs something under her breath.

"I'm Wren's *sister*," she mutters. "I was worried about her."

"Funny way of showing it."

Ellie blows at her bangs again. "Yeah. I guess. It's just...Wren and I have really bad taste in guys. I'm worried Hot—I mean Tate—is going to hurt her."

"Tate's a great guy. She's lucky to have him."

"*She's* lucky?" Ellie wheels around on me, wobbling dangerously on her heels. The club music swings into deep bass line, and she leans forward so I can hear her. "Try *he's* lucky. My sister is amazing."

"So amazing you have to jump her fiancé?"

"There wasn't going to *be* any jumping. I was going to flirt with him to see if he was cheater." Ellie fidgets with her hair, tugging it this way and that. It's distracting as hell. "I had to make sure he's worthy of her. But *now* we'll just have to wait it out. It could take months for his true colors to show."

I pause. *Is it just me or did she make this sound like my fault?* "Your crazy is showing," I say, rolling my bourbon glass from palm to palm. It's no good though. I can still feel her skin against mine. "You might want to tuck that back in."

She rolls her eyes like *I'm* the ass. "You don't understand. She's been hurt too many times."

"Welcome to the real world. It happens."

Ellie looks at me for a long moment—too long actually because it gives me plenty of time to notice how she's exactly the right height to fit under my chin and how her curves look in that fitted dress. Damn. Why am I attracted to wild party girls?

When I left for Dublin, I gave up on two things. One, I swore off girls like Ellie and Mandy. Christ, *Mandy*. We'd been engaged when she slept with that polo player. Kept the ring on and everything. My friends said it was because she was wild. My father said it was because I wasn't enough to keep her still.

Which brings me to the second thing I gave up: my father. I promised myself I didn't need his approval—which was good because I was never going to get it anyway.

And now here I am, back to take over his breeding farm and unable to take my eyes away from Little Miss I Have a Plan.

I can't decide if that makes me pathetic, or incredibly stupid.

"They're getting married," Ellie says finally, glancing away from me. "I hadn't even met him until now."

Wow. Okay, I kinda sorta understand why she's upset. I met Wren weeks ago. I took a few days off from the breeding barn I managed, and flew to Paris for a weekend. We had dinner together and by the time I left, I knew all about Wren's art doctorate, her love for all things French, and the fact she only has one living relative: her sister, Ellie.

Which means I've spent more time with Wren and Tate than she has.

I rattle the ice in my glass. "They're good together."

Ellie shakes her head. "Well, clearly you're the expert."

"You would be too, if you hopped a plane." Although to be honest, the only reason Tate probably brought me in is because A. I'm his best friend and B. no *one* has better radar for crazy than I do.

Actually, B is a bit of a stretch. Tate's so in love with Wren he can't see straight. The girl could be green with scales and he'd be thrilled. Normally, this would be cause for major concern, but after meeting Wren, I couldn't be happier for him. She's straight up amazing. No crazy there.

It all went to her sister instead.

"I'm not an expert on them," I say at last, finishing the last of my bourbon. "I only met Wren last month."

And I suddenly remember how Wren described Ellie as her 'baby sister.' I take another long look at Ellie's curves. Baby sister is definitely not the way I would describe this girl.

I clear my throat. "You'll like Tate. He's great."

"So great she said they would probably move for his job," Ellie says quietly, so quietly I pretend I didn't hear her.

Too bad I can't push it from my mind. She's scared of being left behind. I get that. I don't want to, but I do. When I was growing up, my mom traveled extensively for our farm's breeding program. She was always looking for broodmares with certain bloodlines or stallions with international potential. It was amazing for her, and miserable for me. Left at home, I spent most of my time with my father—the Colonel—and it was horrible. I spent almost ten years plotting my escape.

And now you're back. I sigh, and look around for the waitress again, spotting her on the other side of the dance floor.

"Well?" Ellie asks.

I blink. I have no idea what she's talking about. "Well what?"

"You said you moved back from Ireland. Why?"

"I'm taking over the manager position at a local farm."

"Wait." Ellie turns her head to one side, long brown hair sweeping in a shining curtain across her shoulder. "Caleb...what's your last name?"

"Reese."

She's still staring at Wren, but her expression has hollowed. She looks like she's going to be sick. "Caleb. *Reese.*"

"Yeah."

Those big, brown eyes swing to me, and stick. "Like *Michael* Reese's son?"

I stiffen. "How do you know the Colonel?"

"He owns the place I work at." Her nose wrinkles as she looks me up and down. "You're here for the manager position? I'm your competition for it."

TEASER CHAPTER 3 | Caleb

It takes me five whole seconds before I can form words again. "You're my *what*?" I manage at last.

"I'm your competition for the Jacks or Better job." Ellie straightens her shoulders again, studying me with interest. My body tightens in response. "I know the Colonel told you about me."

"He told me someone else was applying. He didn't tell me she was—was—" I shake myself. "The job is mine, sweetheart. Not only am I his son, but I am very, very good at what I do."

"So am I. *Plus*, I'm the rider who's going to put his homegrown mare in the Grand Prix ring."

I frown. She's got me there. Beckon was the year before I left. The only thing I really remember about the filly was her size (smaller), her color (dark bay, no white), and her attitude (foul). Then, maybe two years ago, the mare started making a name for herself in the lower levels. She won two competitions in Wellington before returning to Jacks or Better for more training. The Colonel thinks she's our best homebred yet, and he very well might be right.

"Cute that you think that matters," I tell her. "Riders are a dime a dozen. Actual professionals? Way more rare."

"Is that what you call sleeping with your father's assistant trainer?"

I go still. It's been six years since I fell for Mandy and that's *still* the first thing everyone remembers? I nearly laugh. Who am I kidding? Of *course* it is. This is the horse industry. Everyone knows everyone and everyone gossips.

I step a little closer, crowding Ellie. "Jealous, sweetheart?"

She blinks. Good. I've caught her off guard. But she's caught me too. This close, I can smell her perfume—something soft and clean—and I can see that amazing cleavage again. Christ, it makes my mouth go hot.

There's a flurry of movement over Ellie's shoulder, and I glance up. Smirk. "I think you may have a problem."

Ellie whips around, spotting the 'problem' right away: her sister's leaving. Wren strides away from Holly like a woman on a mission, and Tate dashes after her, his expression panicked. He should be. If I had any drink left in my glass, I would lift it in solidarity.

Good luck, my man, I think. *You're going to need it.*

"Oh no!" Ellie gasps, and takes off after both of them.

I sigh and follow, Ellie's little friend falling into stride next to me. "Holly," she says in greeting.

I lift my chin. "Caleb."

"Nice to meet you."

I start to ask the curvy blonde if this all seems normal to her—because she's sure as hell acting like it is—and shut my mouth. I don't want to know. I just want to go home.

Outside the club, the air feels like a sauna, humid and overfull with the promise of thunderstorms. Welcome to the south. After so many years of rain and cold, I actually missed it. The sun's been down for hours now, but everything is still warm and close.

Ellie catches Wren underneath a parking lot light and they begin to argue. Tate—probably because he learns faster than I do—stays out of it, hovering at a distance in case his girl needs help.

"Wren, please." Ellie's holding onto her sister's elbow for dear life and Wren keeps trying to shake her off. "I just thought—"

"*No!* You didn't think! You *never* think!" Wren rips herself away, and power stomps to Tate's car. Ellie stares after her, eyes huge and round, and I have the sudden stupid urge to put my arm around her shoulders. Then, as if she feels me staring, Ellie's gaze flicks to me. The haunted look disappears, replaced instead with cool determination. She nods in my direction as if we are about to start a game, which I guess in a way we are.

But not at all like she thinks. Competition for the manager position? Please.

"That actually went better than I expected," Holly announces, but whether she's talking to me or to herself, I can't tell. She turns to me, blonde hair falling around her shoulders. "I guess I'll see you around then, yeah?"

"Not if I see you first."

She laughs, and pats my arm. "You're funny."

Crazy. Both of them. I watch Holly rush to Ellie's side. She leads the other girl toward the line of taxis waiting by the entrance. They don't look back and I can't seem to stop staring.

Why am I still so annoyed?

"Caleb!" Tate waves me toward him, and I gotta say, the guy looks a bit wild-eyed. Poor bastard. I follow him to his car. Wren is already inside, chewing her thumbnail to death. Tate nods his head toward Ellie and Holly. "Think it'll be better by the wedding?" he asks, dropping his voice.

"No."

He pulls a face. "Yeah. Well at least, you don't have to see her before then."

"Ellie? Oh, I'll be seeing her."

Tate throws me a sideways W-T-F look.

"Remember the Colonel saying I had competition for the job?" I ask.

"Yeah."

I glare at Ellie's back as she climbs into her taxi. "Behold my competition."

* * *

Tate drops Wren off at the bed-and-breakfast they're staying at, and drives me out to Jacks or Better. The farm is maybe thirty minutes outside of town, and for once, I'm grateful for the drive. Between the bourbon and the jet lag, I feel like I'm moving underwater. I need time to think, to plan, but every time I close my eyes I see Ellie shimmying closer, and every time I open them, I remember I'm back home.

Tate runs the windows down, and hot, humid air hurls through the BMW. "Tonight was different."

I pause. "You aren't pissed?"

He grunts, and shifts into a lower gear as we take the last bend before the farm's main drive. "Not as much as Wren. I think Ellie just made a bad decision."

"Having the chicken instead of the steak is a bad decision. That was..." I have no words to adequately express that level of bullshit so I wave my hand in a circle. Tate seems to get the idea anyway. He shrugs, making a right into Jacks or Better.

"Seriously," I continue as the smell of fresh cut grass fills the car. "That was a whole new level of crazy. Do you really want to marry into it?"

"Absolutely."

I twist around in my seat, studying Tate's face for signs of lying, but no matter how hard I search, I can't find any. I fling myself back around. He means it. I actually envy that. I've never been that sure about a person—even when Mandy and I were doing well, I was never that sure about her, never that sure about anything.

Actually, no, that's not true. I'm sure I want a future in showjumping. I've shaped my whole life around it: all the work for Jacks or Better, another six years working for two farms outside of Dublin. It's everything I am.

And the deeper we drive into Jacks or Better, the more that realization begins to feel like a death sentence. Coming home wasn't supposed to be like this. I wasn't supposed to be this pissy. I wasn't supposed to fight another employee for the manager job.

I wasn't supposed to play my father's games anymore.

What am I doing here? I wonder, scrubbing both hands over my face. "Did you really not know who Wren's sister was?"

Tate raises his right hand. "Swear to God. I mean, I think Wren mentioned she rode horses, but I pretty much forgot. We got onto oth-er...things."

Part of me wants to be seriously annoyed, but I can't really bring myself to be. Tate and I have been best friends since college. A lot of people in the horse industry don't bother with university, but I want-ed a business degree to better understand how to make a farm work. I knew the day to day stuff, but I wanted—needed—more. If I was going to do better than the Colonel, I figured university was the best way to start. Tate was the same way. Like me, he knew what he wanted: fan-cy job, big house, traveling the world. Unlike me, he isn't walking into an established business. His parents are teachers. They'd give him the world if they could.

Tate drums his fingers along the steering wheel. "I mean, I know we've moved pretty fast, but damn. Didn't realize I'd missed that. The only stuff I remember is Wren's real dad and stepmom died in a car ac-cident so she's all the family Ellie has."

I wince. She's all Ellie's got? And she's leaving? Ouch. "Does she get along with Wren's mom?"

"I don't think they spend a lot of time together. Lynn stays in Paris, and Ellie is supposed to be a workaholic. Wren says she doesn't get out enough."

"Look what happens when she does."

"No shit." Somewhere in the dark, a horse whinnies, and Tate glances at me. "Anyway, who hasn't made bad decisions while drinking peach martinis?"

I eye him. "You think this is funny?"

"Yeah, a bit." He grins, face green from the dashboard lights. "More than a bit. Usually, you would too."

I sit back against the seat, tapping my fingers against my thigh. "No, I wouldn't."

Tate fiddles with the radio, and for a few minutes, there's nothing but the sound of air rushing through the open windows. "Are you okay?"

"You look different today, Dr. Phil."

"And you still look like an asshole. I'm not trying to play therapist. You want to talk? Talk."

Fair enough. I glance out the window. In the dark, the trees are a curtain of shadows rushing by, and as we slow down for the last turn, I can hear the high-pitched whine of crickets. "It's this place, this *town*. It was a mistake."

"You mean coming back?"

"I mean everything. The Colonel calls me, and asks me to come home, and against my better judgment, I agree. I quit my job. I asked Aiden to come on. Then I find out he doesn't want me to take over the farm, he wants me to *interview* to take over the farm. That's bullshit."

"No doubt. But you knew that before you flew over. Why'd you still come?"

"Because it wasn't just me anymore. I had Aiden quit his job at the farm to follow me. He's supposed to ride for Jacks or Better now and he's depending on this as much as I am—more so. He takes care of his sister's kids."

Aiden's also one of the most talented show jumping riders I've ever seen. His feel, his sense of timing, hell his ability to get the most from his horses, blows most riders out of the water. If life were fair, the guy would have sponsors lining up. Since life isn't, he's been coming up through the ranks on his own, getting rides and horses as he can. He was living in his car before coming to my farm last year. This was—*is*—a huge opportunity for him. For both of us.

"That all?" Tate asks.

For two whole seconds, I'm beyond pissed because really does there need to be more? Then I realize what Tate's getting at. "And I want the damn job."

"So get it."

I raise one brow. "At Ellie's expense? Is that what brother-in-laws are supposed to say?"

Tate frowns. "Probably not, but you've wanted this for as long as I've known you. You want it? Go get it."

He pulls to a stop next to the Colonel's Range Rover, and we both take a long look at the house. The antebellum mansion is dark, but one window burns bright. My father's still awake. Waiting for me? God, I hope not. I don't have the energy for one of our arguments.

"Seriously," Tate adds. "There's no way she'd be better at this than you would be. Don't fall for the Colonel's head games."

I crack my knuckles. "It's not just the head games. I'm walking back into that shit I left behind with Mandy."

Tate winces. We've been friends since college and he knows the story. "You know how I felt about Mandy," I say. "But to everyone else, I slept with an employee. They think I used her, and it's *still* following me. Even Ellie threw it in my face."

Tate laughs.

"It's not funny."

"It's totally funny." He turns to me, expression all lawyer-y and composed. "Look, you're not the first guy to break some rules, and get burned. Was Mandy underage?"

"God, no."

"Was she willing?"

"Hell, yes."

"Then what's the deal?"

I grind my teeth. "It made me look like I can't keep my hands off the staff. You should've heard the Colonel's freak out—and when Mandy went public with our drama? It burned my professional standing to the ground."

"So build it back up."

"By standing on your future sister-in-law?" I really can't believe he would suggest it. Tate's a nice guy, an honorable guy, which sounds cheesy as all hell, but it's a big deal to me. He doesn't screw people over.

"Yeah, I know," he says, picking at the leather on his steering wheel. "But Caleb, you're a good boss. You're driven, but you don't ask anyone to do something you wouldn't. Your guys bend over backward for you. I know you'll treat her well."

The compliment makes my skin crawl. Some of that is because I'm no good with niceties. The rest of it is because if—*when*—I make farm manager, I won't treat Ellie nicely at all. I don't need her propensity for drama. I'll fire her.

Enjoyed the excerpt?

...

Get the full version from your favorite book sellers: **emmaashe.com/ books**[1]

---

1. http://www.emmaashe.com/books/deeper

LEAVE A REVIEW

Thanks so much for reading! There are a lot of books out there to choose from, I appreciate you trying mine. Even if you completely hated it (really, really hoping you didn't!), I'm a big believer in the importance of reviews. If you could take a moment to **leave a review**[1] to let everyone know what you think, it would be so appreciated. Not only does it help other readers, but it also helps me become a better writer.

All the love,
    Emma

---

1. http://www.emmaashe.com/books/deeper

ABOUT THE AUTHOR

Hi! I'm Emma and I hate writing about myself in the third person. I write fairly steamy contemporary romance. *Deeper Than Destiny* is the first book in my Deeper Than Love series. I'm having fun with these, and I hope you enjoy them too.

...

Deeper Than Love
Deeper Than Desire, Prequel[1]
Deeper Than Destiny, Book 1[2]
Deeper Than Lies, Book 2[3]
Deeper Than Secrets, Book 3[4]
Deeper Than Temptation, Book 4[5]

An Indecent Apposal
Something Real, Prequel[6]
Show Me Your Secrets, Book 1[7]
Claiming The Secretary, Book 2[8]
Second Chance Romance, Book 3[9]
All For Her, Book 4[10]

---

1. http://www.emmaashe.com/books/deeper

2. http://www.emmaashe.com/books/deeper

3. http://www.emmaashe.com/books/deeper

4. http://www.emmaashe.com/books/deeper

5. http://www.emmaashe.com/books/deeper

6. http://www.emmaashe.com/books/apposal

7. http://www.emmaashe.com/books/apposal

8. http://www.emmaashe.com/books/apposal

9. http://www.emmaashe.com/books/apposal

10. http://www.emmaashe.com/books/apposal

Better With You, Book 5[11]
Anyone But You, Book 6[12]

...

An Indecent Apposal Volume 1, Books 1-3[13]
An Indecent Apposal Volume 2, Books 4-6[14]

...

An Indecent Apposal Collection 1, Books 1-6[15]

Follow me at Emma Ashe Author on Instagram and Facebook or **sign up**[16] for book release announcements, cover reveals, and bonus content.

11. http://www.emmaashe.com/books/apposal

12. http://www.emmaashe.com/books/apposal

13. http://www.emmaashe.com/books/apposal-set

14. http://www.emmaashe.com/books/apposal-set

15. http://www.emmaashe.com/books/apposal-set

16. **http://www.emmaashe.com/signup-book**

www.ingramcontent.com/pod-product-compliance
Lightning Source LLC
Chambersburg PA
CBHW072058170626
46813CB00004B/1407